Warfare in the 18th Century

HISTORY OF WARFARE

Ian Westwell

Steck-Vaughn Company

First published 1999 by Raintree Steck-Vaughn Publishers,
an imprint of Steck-Vaughn Company.
Copyright © 1999 Brown Partworks Limited.

All rights reserved. No part of this book may be used or reproduced in any manner whatsoever or transmitted in any form or by any means, electronic or mechanical, including photocopying, recording, or any information storage and retrieval system, without written permission from the copyright owner except in the case of brief quotations embodied in critical articles and reviews. For information, address the publisher: Steck-Vaughn, P.O. Box 26015, Austin, TX 78755.

Library of Congress Cataloging-in-Publication Data

Westwell, Ian
    Warfare in the 18th century / Ian Westwell.
       p.   cm. — (History of warfare)
    Includes bibliographical references and index.
    Summary: Presents an overview of the major wars of the eighteenth century, an era dominated by conflicts between Europe's leading powers both on the European continent and overseas in the newly established colonies.
    ISBN 0-8172-5445-5
    1. Military history, Modern — 18th century — Juvenile literature.
2. Military art and science — History--18th century — Juvenile literature.
[1. Military history, Modern — 18th century. 2. Military art and science — History — 18th century.] I. Title.
    II. Series.
    D88.W47   1999
    355' .009'034 — dc21
                                                        98-3633
                                                                    CIP
                                                                      AC

Printed and bound in the United States
1 2 3 4 5 6 7 8 9 0 IP 03 02 01 00 99 98

Brown Partworks Limited
Managing Editor: Ian Westwell
Senior Designer: Paul Griffin
Picture Researcher: Wendy Verren
Editorial Assistant: Antony Shaw
Cartographers: William le Bihan, John See
Index: Pat Coward

Raintree Steck-Vaughn
Publishing Director: Walter Kossmann
Project Manager: Joyce Spicer
Editor: Shirley Shalit

Front cover: Prussian troops in Silesia advance against the enemy, 1745 (main picture) and Catherine the Great, empress of Russia (inset).
Page 1: The siege of Fort Detriot by Native American warriors, 1763.

Consultant
Dr. Niall Barr, Senior Lecturer,
Royal Military Academy Sandhurst,
Camberley, Surrey, England

Acknowledgments listed on page 80 constitute part of this copyright page.

Contents

Introduction	4
The Great Northern War	5
The War of the Spanish Succession	12
The War of the Austrian Succession	24
The Jacobite Rebellions	32
Early Native American Wars	34
North America's Anglo–French Wars	38
Europe's Struggle for India	48
The Seven Years War	56
The New Navies	68
Catherine the Great's Wars	72
Glossary and Bibliography	78
Index	79
Acknowledgments	80

Introduction

This volume covers the wars of the 18th century, an era in which conflict was dominated by the rivalries between Europe's leading powers. There were two major areas of war—Europe itself and overseas, in those territories where Europeans were carving out their earliest colonies. Chief among these were North America and India. Apart from those wars fought by powers eager to gain colonies, the main conflicts were fought in Europe by Europe's royal families. Their aim was simple—they wanted to dominate their rivals and control Europe.

The life of the ordinary soldier or sailor during this era was harsh. They were poorly paid and had to suffer hard discipline—beatings and floggings were common. Life on campaign was equally dangerous. Many more soldiers died from illness or disease than suffered death in battle. Men wounded in battle received little medical attention and minor wounds were often fatal. Perhaps unsurprisingly rates of desertion among the ordinary soldiers were high. Few commanders could count on their army's strength in the field being maintained for any length of time.

There was not a great deal of military innovation during this period. Weapons, tactics, and levels of generalship evolved slowly. Infantry continued to move in rigid columns and then deploy in lines two or more men deep to fight at usually very close ranges. Infantrymen, however, were increasingly able to defeat cavalry. The pike, for a long time the best means for infantry to stop cavalry, finally disappeared at the beginning of the century as the bayonet was introduced to give the musket-carrying infantry the ability to protect themselves. Artillery was becoming standardized and much more mobile, allowing guns to dominate battlefields with their firepower and range. Artillery was becoming the biggest killer of soldiers in action.

Soldiers were expected to perform certain maneuvers and fight in close ranks on the battlefield. Their tactics and drills were practiced frequently in peacetime and every soldier and officer knew what was expected of him—obedience and discipline, and the ability to follow orders in the heat of battle. As the effective range of muskets was low, firefights were at very close range. Artillery and musket fire quickly clouded battlefields in smoke due to the use of smoke-producing gunpowder. Soldiers had to wear standardized and usually bright clothing so that friends and foes could be more easily identified through the "fog" of battle.

The great generals of the time saw that their armies were roughly equal in quality and tried to maneuver their forces to put an enemy at a disadvantage, either in difficult terrain or far away from support or a friendly supply base. The best commanders of the period were Frederick the Great of Prussia and Britain's Duke of Marlborough. Both had a superb grasp of strategy and frequently put their enemies at a disadvantage by the speed of their armies' movement.

The Great Northern War

By the end of the 17th century Sweden was widely regarded as the major power in the Baltic Sea area. It was a situation that other powers in the region—chiefly Denmark, Poland, and Russia—found unacceptable. Believing that they could take advantage of the youth and inexperience of King Charles XII of Sweden, these three allies attacked in April 1700, sparking the Great Northern War. Charles had a small but well-trained army, but surely he could not take on and defeat the combined might of Denmark, Poland, and Russia?

The Danes struck first, successfully conquering a Swedish ally. The Poles also invaded and placed the Swedish city of Riga (now the capital of Latvia) under siege. The Russians, led by Peter the Great, besieged the Swedish port city of Narva (now in Estonia). Charles made the decision to deal with Denmark first.

Going against the advice of his more experienced officers, Charles made a bold move. Taking his army and fleet across some supposedly unnavigable waters, he threatened Copenhagen, the Danish capital. The Danes, caught off guard by Charles's unexpected action, asked for peace, agreeing to end hostilities with Sweden.

Charles takes on Poland

With one of his three enemy allies out of the way, Charles next planned to deal with the Poles outside Riga. However, he soon changed his mind and decided to advance against the Russians. His small army—some 8,000 men—brushed aside a Russian force outside Narva on November 18, 1700, and two days later took on the bulk of the Russian forces. The Battle of Narva, fought in a snowstorm, was short and bloody. In less than two hours the Russians, who outnumbered Charles by nearly five-to-one, were cut to pieces by the Swedes. Riga itself was relieved by the Swedes in June 1701. The Russians and Poles retreated in confusion.

Charles XII, king of Sweden from 1697 until his death in action in 1718, was a shrewd battlefield general. However, he underestimated the strength of his rivals in Eastern Europe.

Charles, believing that Russia was now the lesser threat, moved to knock seemingly stronger Poland out of the war. The Swedes invaded in early July, defeating a Russian army that stood in their way at the Battle of Dunamunde (now in Lithuania) on the 9th. Fighting stopped during the winter, but Charles began his advance again in the new year, occupying the Polish capital, Warsaw, on May 14, 1702. Despite capturing Warsaw, Charles continued to campaign against Poland until 1706.

These campaigns were almost wholly successful. In battle after battle Charles defeated his opponents. On September 24, 1706, the Polish monarch, Augustus II, was forced to give up his throne and cancel his alliance with Russia. Peter the Great of Russia, having now lost his two allies, offered to sign a peace treaty. Charles, however, was bent on revenge and, displaying the pigheadedness that would eventually bring about his downfall, refused the Russian peace offer.

Looking back, Charles's decision to concentrate his efforts against Poland can be seen as a mistake. Despite their catastrophic defeat at Narva, the Russians could draw on huge reserves of manpower. While Charles campaigned against Poland,

The Battle of Narva was fought between the Swedes and Russians in November 1700. The Swedes, attacking in a freezing snowstorm, smashed the Russians in just two hours.

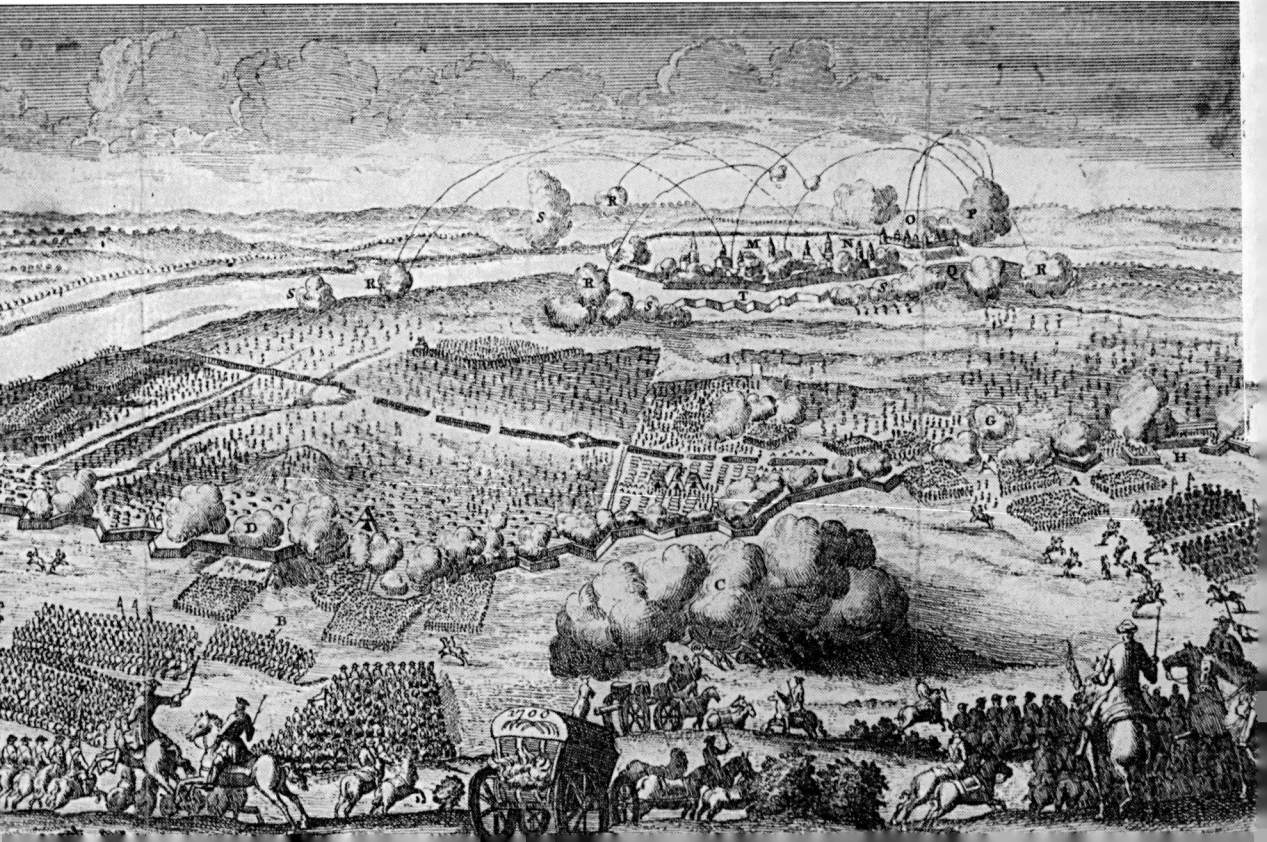

the Russians were able to train a new army and even recaptured Narva in August 1704. All of the city's Swedish inhabitants were massacred by the Russians.

Charles still thirsted to crush the Russians. On January 1, 1708, he took advantage of several frozen rivers that when flowing made any advance difficult to lead his army of 45,000 men against the Russians. At first the invasion went well. Charles pushed the Russians back toward their homeland, inflicting a defeat on them at Holowczyn in eastern Poland on July 4. However, Charles was unable to bring the main Russian army to battle.

The Russians avoid battle

The Russians knew that they could not match the Swedes in open battle for the moment. Despite their superior numbers, the Russians were inferior soldiers compared with Charles's battle-hardened veterans. Peter the Great played a waiting game. He ordered the main Russian army to avoid battle, to retreat, and leave behind nothing of value to the Swedes. As Charles advanced deeper into Russia after his victory at Holowczyn, he crossed a land in which crops and fodder had been destroyed. As he moved farther and farther from his bases, his army ran short of supplies. Hunger, intense cold, and disease began to thin the Swedish ranks. By October 1708 Charles and his dwindling army were in real difficulty.

Charles should have either halted to allow supplies to be brought forward or retreated. He did neither. Instead, he swung southward and headed for the Ukraine in the deep south of Russia. He intended to get supplies from the local cossack tribes and forge an alliance with them against the Russians. Charles also ordered one of his generals, Adam Loewenhaupt, to march south to join him in the Ukraine. Loewenhaupt was told to gather as many supplies as he could before setting off. If Loewenhaupt failed to reach Charles with the supplies, the Swedes would be cut off hundreds of miles from home.

Peter the Great ruled Russia from 1672 until his death in 1725. A ruthless, dynamic ruler, he dragged Russia into the modern world. Peter rebuilt the Russian navy, curbed the power of rebellious nobles, and founded a beautiful new capital, St. Petersburg.

Warfare in the 18th Century

The Russians moved quickly and decisively to make sure that Charles's plans would fail. Peter the Great ordered an army to advance into the Ukraine and put the cossack capital to the torch. The threat of a cossack rebellion was smashed by this decisive action. Another Russian army was earmarked to attack Loewenhaupt's supply column as it moved to link up with Charles. In a two-day battle in early October 1708 Loewenhaupt was defeated. Loewenhaupt and roughly half of his 11,000 Swedish troops escaped to link up with Charles on the 21st, but the precious supplies were abandoned or destroyed.

Charles's fortunes did not improve. The winter of 1708–1709 was the coldest in living memory. The Swedish army was being ground down. By the beginning of spring Russian harassing attacks, lack of food, and intense cold had reduced Charles's force to about 25,000 men. The Swedes were short of powder and shot for their muskets and fewer than 40 cannon remained in working order.

If complete defeat was to be avoided Charles need a decisive victory. He hoped that he could draw the Russian army into a battle by besieging the city of Poltava in southern Russia. Peter seemed to have taken the bait. He advanced on Poltava with 80,000 men and more than 100 cannon. The two armies sized each other up and skirmishes took place. During one Charles was wounded in the foot.

Gambling on an attack

As the Russians grew stronger, the Swedes were wasting away. Charles, though vastly outnumbered, decided to attack on June 28. Showing their usual courage and professionalism, the Swedish troops made considerable progress, chiefly against a number of fortifications the Russians had built to protect their poor-quality infantry and slow any Swedish attack. Victory seemed within Charles's grasp. One more

CHARLES XII OF SWEDEN

Born in 1682 Charles was not quite 19 years old when he succeeded to the Swedish throne after his father died. Charles was an intelligent and resourceful general. He had to fight Denmark, Poland, and Russia whose combined military might was much more than Sweden's.

Charles had two advantages. First, he led a skilled, highly professional, and well-motivated army that, although small, was considerably more effective than his opponents'. Second, he was a superior strategist. He planned to move rapidly, before his enemies could combine, and defeat them one by one. This he almost accomplished.

If he had agreed to peace terms with Russia in 1706, after he had dealt with Denmark and Poland, Charles would have made sure that Sweden was as powerful as Russia. However, his decision to continue the war against Russia was a fateful mistake, one that would end Sweden's attempted domination of the Baltic Sea area.

THE GREAT NORTHERN WAR

A cossack cavalryman. from southern Russia. He is mounted on a sturdy pony and is equipped with a lance and saber. The cossacks were a fiercely independent people. They did not like the attempts of Peter the Great to make them part of the growing Russian Empire.

push, Charles believed, and the Russians would break. However, his first attacks had been spread out and his forces were unable to deliver a coordinated charge.

Peter mustered his remaining forces—some 40,000 men—to meet the Swedish onslaught. About 7,000 Swedes made the attack. Blasted by musket and cannon fire, the Swedes were halted in their tracks and then their formation disintegrated. What was once one of the best armies in Europe was changed into a fleeing rabble. The Swedes suffered close to 10,000 men killed and had over 15,000 captured. The Russians lost less than 5,000 troops in total. Charles, with a small group of cavalrymen, fled into Turkish-controlled territory to the south of Poltava.

Sweden's Turkish allies

The Russians moved westward to liberate Poland and put Augustus II back on the throne. The three allies—Denmark, Poland, and Russia—also set about capturing Swedish territories. However, Charles was far from idle. From his refuge he persuaded the Turks to declare war on the Russians in October 1710.

A Turkish army of 200,000 troops gathered along the south Russian border. Peter the Great, at the head of 60,000 men, moved to deal with the Turkish threat. Overconfidence, born out of his success at Poltava, proved to be his downfall. Peter was outmaneuvered and forced to surrender in 1711. The Turks, however, offered generous peace terms—much to Charles's disgust.

Russian and Swedish cavalry clash during the Battle of Poltava in June 1709. The battle was decided when the Swedish infantry was shot to pieces by the Russians as they launched a last, desperate attack.

THE GREAT NORTHERN WAR

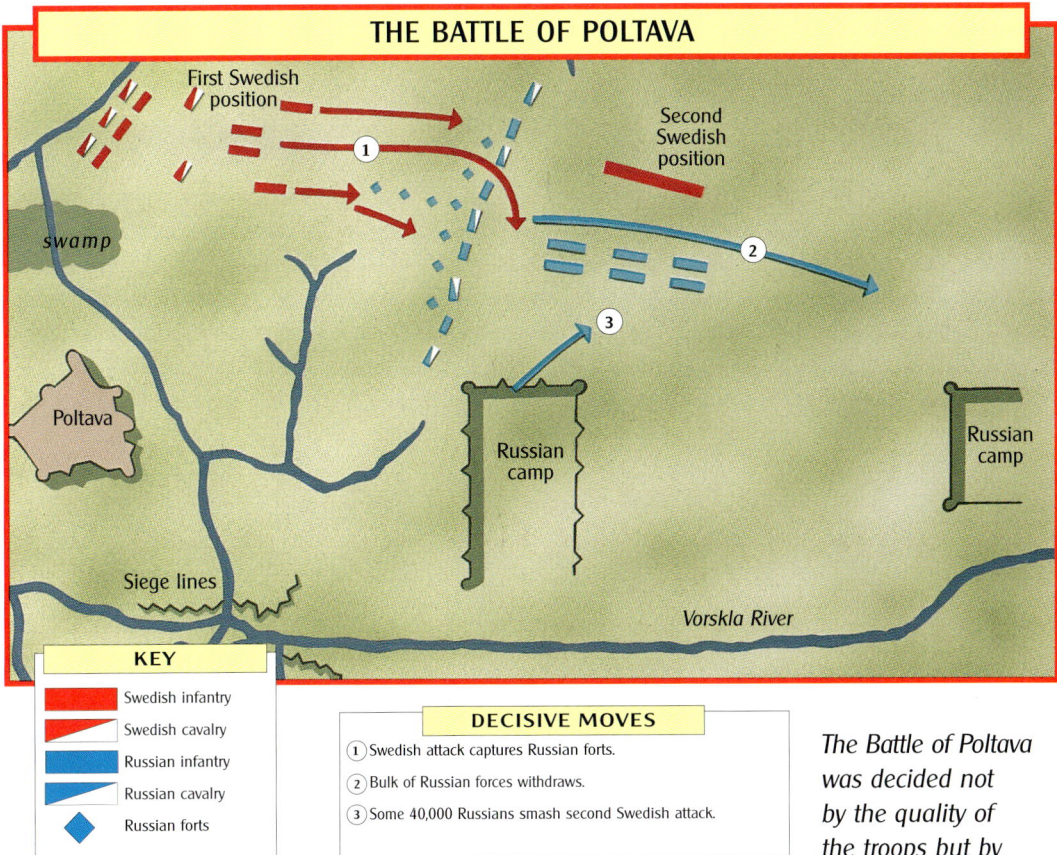

The Battle of Poltava was decided not by the quality of the troops but by numbers. The Russian army was much larger than that of Sweden. The 20,000 Swedes, although the better soldiers, were not able to overcome odds of about four-to-one.

Although it was clear that his hopes of Turkey continuing to fight Russia were dashed, Charles continued to propose war. The Turks became so sick of Charles's actions that they placed him under house arrest. Charles, however, escaped and returned to Sweden in November 1714.

Sweden was under great threat but Charles's arrival seemed to give new life to his country. He quickly raised an army of 20,000 men and was able to block an invasion of Sweden by 1716. He now took the war to the enemy, invading Norway, then controlled by Denmark, in 1717. However, on December 11, 1718, he was killed while besieging the city of Fredriksten in Norway.

The war continued for a few more years until the signing of the Treaty of Nystad, a city now in Finland, in August 1721. The peace confirmed that Sweden had been replaced by Russia as the major power in the Baltic. Charles had proved himself a greater leader of men in battle but a poor leader of a country at war.

11

The War of the Spanish Succession

The War of the Spanish Succession, fought from 1701 to 1714, was sparked by squabbles over who was the rightful heir to the Spanish throne. King Charles of Spain died childless in November 1700 and two rival monarchs stepped forward—Louis XIV of France and Leopold I of Austria. Both kings wanted one of their relatives on the Spanish throne. Several other European states did not want Spain to be controlled by France or Austria. Whichever controlled Spain (eventually France) would be the strongest power in Europe.

The war began with a French invasion of the Spanish-controlled Netherlands in March 1701. Austria, which also had claims on the region, responded by massing an army under Prince Eugene. The French moved into Italy, then controlled by Austria. Eugene blocked the French, defeating them at the Battle of Chiari in

Prince Eugene of Austria was one of the most outstanding commanders of the War of the Spanish Succession. His greatest strength, however, was his excellent partnership with Britain's Duke of Marlborough. Together the two generals made an almost unbeatable pair.

THE WAR OF THE SPANISH SUCCESSION

northern Italy on September 1. Those countries opposed to French ambitions formed the so-called Grand Alliance less than a week later. Austria allied with England, the Netherlands, Prussia and a host of other German states, and was later joined by Portugal. France formed links with the Italian states of Savoy and Mantua and the German state of Bavaria.

Marlborough takes command

Britain declared war on France on May 15, 1702, and immediately sent General John Churchill to take charge of the British and Dutch forces in the Netherlands. His early operations were somewhat hampered by the Dutch authorities' unwillingness to grant him absolute control over their troops.

Nevertheless, while Eugene continued to battle successfully against the French in Italy, Churchill launched an operation to secure the lower parts of the Rhine and Meuse Rivers where they flowed into the North Sea. A number of cities fell to Churchill between September and October. Churchill was given the title of Duke of Marlborough. The only setback for the Grand Alliance was the defeat of an army from the German state of Baden by the French under General Claude de Villars at the Battle of Friedlingen on October 14. Villars was given the rank of marshal.

French troops dressed in the uniforms worn during the War of the Spanish Succession. Infantrymen wore white or light gray coats with various facing colors on their cuffs and elsewhere. These indicated the particular regiment to which they belonged.

13

Marlborough's strategy was straightforward, if very ambitious. He planned to lead his army down the Rhine to establish links with the Austrians and then retake the French-held forts in the Spanish Netherlands. Antwerp was his ultimate objective. The French were planning to march on Vienna, the Austrian capital.

Marlborough succeeded in gaining a route into the Rhine region thanks to the capture of Bonn in May 1703, but failed to take Antwerp. The French had built up a massive force to prevent this. The main French attack on Vienna began well. Their commander, Marshal de Villars, defeated two Grand Alliance forces at two battles in southern Germany, Munderkingen and Hochstadt. However, one of France's allies, Bavaria, was unwilling to cooperate further, and after a quarrel, Villars resigned his command.

Despite the failure of their march on Vienna, the French maintained their attacks on the Grand Alliance in the second half of 1703. One of their generals, Marshal Camille de Tallard, attacked across the Rhine, taking a German frontier fortress in September and threatening to attack Austria from southern Germany. Winter ended operations, however.

Reconsidering strategy

Winter gave both sides time to reconsider their war strategies. The French decided to focus their efforts in 1704 on Vienna, doing no more than keeping Marlborough occupied in the Netherlands. For his part Marlborough planned a diversionary attack on Spain and also ordered a naval force to attack the French Mediterranean port of Toulon. He planned for the bulk of his forces to accomplish three difficult tasks—save Vienna from capture, drive the French out of Germany, and make sure that Bavaria ended its alliance with France.

By April 1704 France and its allies had over 80,000 troops in Bavaria, while the Austrians could muster about 70,000 men. However, Marlborough was moving down the Rhine with some 35,000 men. It was the Grand Alliance's intention to unite its forces; the French hoped to defeat them before they could link up. By hasty marches that completely outwitted the French, Prince Eugene joined Marlborough on August 12 at Blenheim, a small village a little way to the north of the Danube River. Marlborough's march had also completely outfoxed the French.

The two forces were evenly matched. Marlborough and Eugene led 56,000 troops; while the French and their Bavarian allies numbered a little more, about 60,000. Marlborough began

THE WAR OF THE SPANISH SUCCESSION

THE BATTLE OF BLENHEIM

Fought on August 13, 1704, Blenheim (see also map page 21) was Marlborough's greatest victory. The battle against the French began with Prince Eugene attacking the French left wing and a British column attacking the French forces in Blenheim. These were not meant to be decisive. They were designed to force the French commander, Marshal Camille de Tallard, to bring in his reserves.

Tallard was rattled by the two attacks and did draw in his reserves. Most were drawn into Blenheim. The fighting around the village was bitter, and the British lost heavily. However, Marlborough's prime objective was achieved.

With the French reserves fully occupied, Marlborough unleashed his cavalry against the French center in the late afternoon. The French fought back stubbornly for an hour but finally gave way under the onslaught. Tallard was captured and his men ran for their lives. A total catastrophe was avoided only because a portion of Tallard's army managed to escape before Marlborough was able to complete an encircling maneuver against the French.

The tactics Marlborough used at Blenheim were so devastating that he used them as a plan of action for his other great victories during the War of the Spanish Succession.

The Battle of Blenheim was a catastrophic defeat for the French. They had over 38,000 men killed, wounded, or taken prisoner out of an army of some 60,000 men.

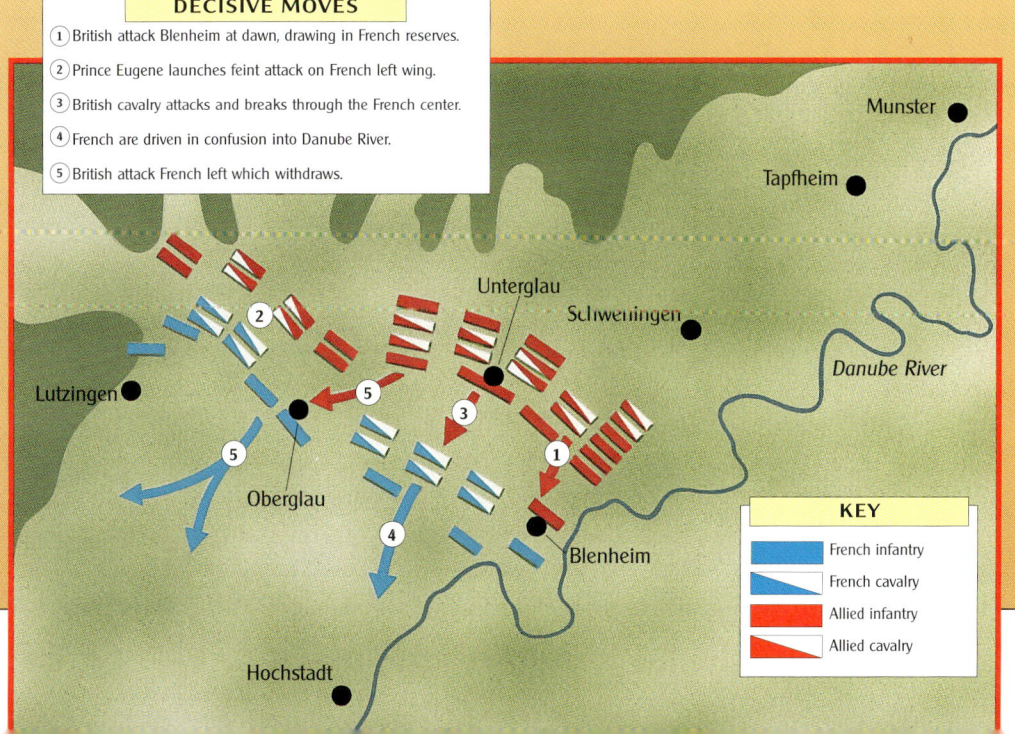

DECISIVE MOVES
1. British attack Blenheim at dawn, drawing in French reserves.
2. Prince Eugene launches feint attack on French left wing.
3. British cavalry attacks and breaks through the French center.
4. French are driven in confusion into Danube River.
5. British attack French left which withdraws.

KEY
- French infantry
- French cavalry
- Allied infantry
- Allied cavalry

The Duke of Marlborough (mounted at right) looks on as his troops break through the French right-wing defenses at the climax of the Battle of Ramillies fought on May 23, 1706.

to deploy for battle early in the morning of the 13th, hoping to catch the French and Bavarians off balance. Because of the nature of the ground Eugene's troops took a little longer to get into position. However, by midday the Grand Alliance forces were drawn up in their battle lines.

The Battle of Blenheim began a little after midday. Marlborough and Eugene won an overwhelming victory and came close to wiping out their opponents. The French and Bavarians suffered horrific casualties—nearly 40,000 killed, wounded, and taken prisoner. Many drowned as they struggled to escape across the Danube. Marlborough lost about 12,000 men killed and wounded. Blenheim was a shattering defeat for France. Bavaria was taken over by the victorious Austrians.

The following year, 1705, was marked by inconclusive maneuverings as both sides sought to gain an advantageous position. In 1706, Marlborough, back in the Netherlands, won his second great victory over the French at the Battle of Ramillies. The battle was brought about because the French believed that Marlborough was intent on capturing Namur and sent 60,000 troops under Marshal François de Villeroi to protect the city.

Villeroi, no match for Marlborough, was stopped on his march to Namur at Ramillies and drew his 60,000 men up in a long, partly fortified line that ran across high ground. Villeroi had no intention of attacking. It was up to Marlborough to push the French back. Marlborough's tactics were masterpieces of coordination. He used some of his 60,000 troops to suggest that he intended to crush the French left wing. Marlborough hoped that Villeroi would move his reserves from the center and right of the French line to reinforce the left wing. The ruse worked.

Next, Marlborough unleashed his main attack against the weakened French right. The French fought stubbornly but were overwhelmed. Seeing the decisive moment had arrived, Marlborough order an advance of his whole army. The French, with losses totaling 15,000 men, were swept from the battlefield. Marlborough suffered fewer than 5,000 casualties.

Vital fortresses fall

Ramillies had important results. First, it led to the dismissal of Villeroi, who was replaced by the more able Louis Josef, Duke de Vendôme. Second, Marlborough's victory allowed him to capture a number of key fortresses, along with thousands of enemy troops. Third, Vendôme had been fighting in northern Italy against Austria's Prince Eugene. Vendôme's departure to take on Marlborough in August 1706 had disastrous consequences for the French campaign in northern Italy.

Eugene was outnumbered by two-to-one and faced an enemy that was behind fortifications, attempting to capture the important city of Turin. Nevertheless he decided to attack an isolated section of the French fortifications on September 7. The fighting was bitter, but a sudden attack by the Turin garrison decided the day. The French were hit from two directions and broke. They fled back to France and their few remaining garrisons in northern Italy had surrendered by the end of the year.

Marlborough and Eugene unite

Both sides maneuvered for advantage throughout 1707, although with little result. Vendôme faced Marlborough in what is now Belgium, but no major battles took place. The only significant action was the campaign by the French who made a lightning strike into southern Germany.

The following year, 1708, saw both sides attempt to gain the upper hand. Marlborough, with 70,000 men, planned to link up with Eugene's 35,000 troops, who would march north from central Germany once a Grand Alliance army had arrived to take his place. For his part Vendôme decided to move first. Between May

John Churchill, Duke of Marlborough

John Churchill, the Duke of Marlborough.

John Churchill, Duke of Marlborough, is widely recognized as one of the greatest commanders of all time. Nicknamed "Corporal John" by his troops, Marlborough fought in an age when armies were slow moving and inflexible and generally unable to move far from fortified supply bases. All that was expected of soldiers was that they stand in ranks and fire close-range volleys. Clever, complicated maneuvers, both on the battlefield and on campaign, were rare.

Marlborough knew that his infantry would fight in the accepted manner, so he needed to try something else to gain an advantage. He chose movement. He repeatedly broke with tradition, moving quickly, often dispensing with supply bases to catch the enemy off balance.

He also used coordinated maneuvers on the battlefield to a greater degree than was usual. At each of his great victories, those at Blenheim, Ramillies, Oudenarde, and Malplaquet, he used false attacks to trick the French into drawing on their reserves. He then launched his main force against a weak spot in the enemy line.

Marlborough also had one other great advantage over the French. Prince Eugene, present at many of his victories, was a superb general in his own right and was always willing to carry out Marlborough's orders to the letter.

and June Vendôme tried to outmaneuver Marlborough. In this he had some success, capturing Ghent and Bruges in July. However, Vendôme knew that time was running out. If he did not bring Marlborough to battle soon, Eugene would arrive from central Germany, making his task all the more difficult.

Marlborough, perhaps surprisingly, was also eager for battle, although Eugene's army had yet to arrive. Two matters concerned him. First, he recognized that Vendôme held the initiative. Second, the morale of the Dutch was shaky. He needed a swift victory to steady his wavering allies. Eugene, who had raced ahead of his army to be with Marlborough, agreed.

The French stand and fight

Marlborough moved quickly. His army covered an astonishing 28 miles (45 km) in less than a day—a remarkable feat for the time. By July 11 Marlborough's men were within sight of the French. One of Vendôme's generals suggested a withdrawal but Vendôme chose to fight. He realized that a retreat might lead to his losing his lines of communications with France.

Vendôme deployed his forces along the high ground to the north of Oudenarde. Both sides chose to attack in the middle of the afternoon. The battle lacked the great skill and cleverness of either Blenheim or Ramillies. What counted was firmness of command, cool nerves under fire, and the discipline of the troops. Again, Marlborough and Eugene proved the better and their forces gained the upper hand. Marlborough was able to get behind the French right wing while Eugene kept the pressure on the front of the French line. Suddenly, at about dusk, the French broke. They had about 18,000 casualties, and 3,000 men deserted. Marlborough suffered less than 10,000 casualties.

Marlborough's victory at Oudenarde and the arrival of Eugene's army gave him a numerical advantage over the French. He had some 120,000 men to oppose the 96,000-strong French army. Marlborough planned to invade France itself but was prevented from doing so by his wary Dutch allies. Instead, he sidestepped Vendôme and laid siege to Lille in August. Vendôme attempted to counter this move by making his own advance against Brussels (now the capital of Belgium), but was forced back by Marlborough, who left Eugene to continue the siege of Lille. The fortress-city fell to Eugene on December 11.

Abandoning military logic

Armies usually ceased campaigning with the onset of winter. Marlborough, however, chose this moment to abandon accepted military logic. He chose to push the French, who probably expected winter would give them an opportunity to gather their strength for the coming year, out of parts of Belgium. Ghent and

Warfare in the 18th Century

Bruges fell to Marlborough in January 1709. Satisfied with these gains, Marlborough decided to stop campaigning until the spring. His army went into winter quarters.

As the weather improved Marlborough had two options. The French were seemingly unwilling to give battle, unless Marlborough was foolish enough to attack them behind their fortifications. Marlborough reasoned that he had either to avoid battle and bypass the French or force them to leave their fortifications. Marlborough reckoned that he could push the French out from behind their fortifications by besieging French-held towns and cities. Tournai fell to his forces on July 29 and he then moved against the fortress-city of Mons. The French feared losing Mons and ordered Villars to march against Marlborough, thereby leaving the safety of their defenses.

Villars led some 90,000 men to take up position at Malplaquet, where they hastily built a line of fortifications. Marlborough responded to the threat by leaving 20,000 men to keep the pressure on Mons and leading 90,000 of his and Eugene's troops to confront the French. The two forces met on September 11.

The plan devised by Marlborough and Eugene reflected the success they had enjoyed at Blenheim and Ramillies. Eugene was to attack the French right, while Marlborough was to attack the left. However, these were not to be the main onslaughts. They were designed to force Villars to use his reserves, thereby severely weakening the French center. The battle was much more severe than either Blenheim or Ramillies, however.

Two diversionary attacks

The two diversionary attacks were launched but the fighting was confused. Villars was so badly wounded that he had to give up his command and Eugene suffered two wounds. The French did weaken their center and Marlborough launched what he hoped would be the deciding attack. The French broke under the

English infantry storms a French fort during the Battle of Malplaquet on September 11, 1709. The infantrymen in conical hats at left are grenadiers. Usually larger, stronger men, they were trained to attack fortifications and used an early form of grenade, hence their name.

THE WAR OF THE SPANISH SUCCESSION

✗ Battles
1. Friedlingen 1702
2. Bonn 1703
3. Munderkingen 1703
4. Hochstadt 1703
5. Blenheim 1704
6. Ramillies 1706
7. Ghent 1708/09
8. Bruges 1708/09
9. Oudenarde 1708
10. Lille 1708
11. Brussels 1708
12. Tournai 1709
13. Mons 1709
14. Malplaquet 1709
15. Denain 1712

onslaught but were able to reform their line. Marlborough committed the last of his reserves to the center of the battle and made the decisive breakthrough.

For all Marlborough and Eugene's skills as commanders Malplaquet was a close-run battle, one decided by the fighting spirit of the ordinary soldier. The ordinary soldiers paid in blood to achieve victory. Marlborough lost over 20,000 men killed and wounded. Villars' force had about 14,000 casualties. Mons, without hope of rescue, was captured on October 26.

The Grand Alliance under threat

The second half of 1710 was taken up with both sides maneuvering to gain some strategic advantage. However, the Grand Alliance was beginning to fall apart. The chief cause of this was a proposal to make the Austrian emperor, Charles VI, the king of Spain. None of the Grand Alliance members, who had gone to war to prevent a monarch ruling over two countries in the first place, wanted one to emerge from their own ranks.

The Grand Alliance also lost its best commander. Marlborough had benefited from the support of Queen Anne of England. But he lost her support and a new government looked less favorably on the general. He was recalled at the end of 1711. Peace negotiations overshadowed the war during 1712.

The War of the Spanish Succession was fought chiefly in the Low Countries (modern Belgium, Luxembourg, and the Netherlands), along the line of the Rhine River, and in the south. Although there were several battles, much of the fighting centered on capturing frontier fortresses.

Eugene attempted to take on Villars and his 100,000 men in May, but he was hindered by the unwillingness of his Dutch allies to fight. Nor did he know that Marlborough's replacement, James Butler, Duke of Ormonde, was under strict orders not to attack the French. Ormonde and his British forces were ordered home, leaving Eugene with not enough troops to mount a meaningful offensive or even to hold onto the gains won shortly before Marlborough was recalled.

The war ends

The French sensed Eugene's weakness and were eager to negotiate peace from a position of strength. Villars caught a portion of Eugene's army by surprise at the Battle of Denain on July 24 and then recaptured a number of the recently lost fortresses. The Treaty of Utrecht was agreed to by all—except the Austrians—in April 1713. Britain gained Newfoundland and other parts of Canada from France, but recognized the right of French-born

French troops led by Marshal Claude de Villars storm fortifications held by Dutch troops during the Battle of Denain on July 24, 1712.

THE WAR OF THE SPANISH SUCCESSION

QUEEN ANNE'S WAR

Although the decisive theater of the War of the Spanish Succession was in Europe, there was considerable fighting in the New World, chiefly in the Caribbean and North America. In these areas the conflict was known as Queen Anne's War. Queen Anne was the ruler of England during the fighting, which lasted from 1702 to 1713.

The war in North America was fought by allies France and Spain against the English. All three had colonies in the area, and used their own colonists and Native Americans during their campaigns.

Between 1702 and 1704 fighting was concentrated in the south of North America. In 1702 English colonists from the Carolinas and Native Americans attacked the Spanish town of St. Augustine. The town fell but the Spanish garrison retreated to a fort and held off the attackers, who withdrew when Spanish warships arrived on the scene. Between 1703 and 1704 both sides carried out hit-and-run raids against isolated settlements and missions.

In the north the French raided English colonial settlements from Maine to Connecticut, and twice launched major operations against Newfoundland (1704 and 1708).

English colonial forces twice tried to capture Port Royal in French-controlled Nova Scotia in 1704 and 1707, but failed. Port Royal was eventually taken by 4,000 British troops backed by warships on October 16, 1710, and renamed Annapolis Royal after the queen. In July 1711 colonists and British troops attempted to take Montreal and Quebec, but the campaign was abandoned after several transport ships sank after hitting rocks in the St. Lawrence River.

Queen Anne's War ended with the signing of the Treaty of Utrecht in 1713. The British gained the most from the treaty. France had to give up its control of Nova Scotia and Newfoundland to Britain and the British won the right to supply African slaves to the Spanish colonies in North America.

Philip V to the throne of Spain. France gave guarantees that the Spanish and French thrones would remain separate. The Spanish were forced to give up their possessions in the Netherlands and most of those in Italy to Austria.

Eugene and Villars continued their increasingly pointless war for several months, but with less and less conviction. The French captured a few fortresses along the Rhine. Hostilities were officially ended by the Treaties of Rastatt and Baden in 1714. These were in many ways similar to the Treaty of Utrecht, although the Austrians refused outright to accept a member of the French royal house on the Spanish throne.

The War of the Austrian Succession

The War of the Austrian Succession, fought between 1740 and 1748, was brought about by a dispute over who should take over the Austrian throne after the death of Charles VI, the Hapsburg ruler of Austria, in 1740. Charles died without any male heirs but had made provision for his eldest daughter, Maria Theresa, to become monarch. This was accepted by many European countries. However, other monarchs, those of Bavaria, Spain, and Saxony, believed they had a better claim than Maria Theresa.

King Frederick II of Prussia, known today as Frederick the Great, sided with Maria Theresa and offered his support. However, this had strings attached. Frederick wanted the Austrian province of Silesia (now southwest Poland). The Austrians refused and Frederick invaded in early 1741. The Austrians were at first ill-prepared to deal with the invasion and the Prussians (who lived in what is now part of eastern Germany) quickly overran the province, except for a few bottled-up Austrian garrisons.

Empress Maria Theresa was not recognized as the legitimate ruler of Austria by certain European kings. They were willing to go to war to dispute her right to rule.

Austria fights back

The Austrians, however, were planning a surprise blow. In the depths of winter, at a time when Frederick had dispersed his army into its winter quarters, the Austrians crossed the snow-covered passes of the Sudeten Mountains into Silesia. Frederick's lines of communication with Prussia were threatened. Frederick was nevertheless equal to the challenge. Gathering his scattered army, he confronted the Austrians at Mollwitz in southern Prussia on April 10.

The battle began badly for Frederick. A charge by the Austrian cavalry against his right-wing cavalry, swept both him and his men from the field. However, one of Frederick's generals launched the Prussian infantry, the best in Europe, against the Austrians. The Austrian army collapsed, leaving the battlefield to the Prussians.

THE WAR OF THE AUSTRIAN SUCCESSION

The War of the Austrian Succession was fought in two main areas. In the east most of the battles took place between the Oder and Elbe Rivers. In the west, the rival armies campaigned along the border between the Holy Roman Empire and France.

After Mollwitz the war dragged in other European countries. Charles Albert of Bavaria, a claimant to the Austrian throne, invaded Austria. His French allies cooperated by moving into southern Germany. Saxony and the Italian state of Savoy also sided with Bavaria. Britain and the Netherlands backed Austria.

The Bavarians and French invaded Austria during the summer of 1741 and then attacked Bohemia in October. They were hoping for the support of Frederick, but the Prussian ruler had signed a secret truce with the Austrians. He gained control of Silesia, but the truce allowed the Austrians to concentrate their forces against the Bavarians and French. The truce was not destined to last. Maria Theresa believed that her army could take on the Bavarians and French, and recover Silesia from Frederick.

Hard-fought victory

Austrian forces invaded Bavaria on December 27, capturing the capital, Munich. The Bavarian army in Bohemia rushed home to confront the Austrians. The smaller French army was unable to attack the Austrians from Bohemia with much hope of success. It was left to Frederick's Prussians to tackled the Austrians. His hard-fought victory at Chotusitz on May 17, 1742, forced Maria Theresa to sign a peace treaty that gave Silesia to Frederick.

25

The war between the Franco-Bavarian forces in Bohemia and southern Germany and the Austrians continued. There was much maneuvering by both sides in late 1742 and the following spring. The Austrians gained the upper hand. The French were forced out of Bohemia in December and the French and Bavarians retreated from Bavaria after their defeat at Braunau in May 1743.

The focal point of the war now switched to northern Europe, where King George II, the last British monarch to lead an army in person, gathered a multinational force of 40,000 men and advanced down the Rhine River. The French moved a force of 30,000 to block George. The two armies met at Dettingen on June 27. George, although brave, was no military genius. A French cavalry charge almost smashed the British left wing. George, without his horse which had bolted, drew his sword and personally led his infantry into the attack on foot. The maneuver worked and the French withdrew after hard fighting. Remarkably, the two countries had not yet declared war.

France and Britain did declare war in April 1744. Three French armies were prepared for action. One prepared to invade the Netherlands. Another, later commanded by Marshal Maurice de Saxe, was positioned along the straight middle portions of the

King George II (center) rallies his British infantry for one final attack against the French army during the Battle of Dettingen on June 27, 1743.

MARSHAL DE SAXE

In an age in which original military thought was in short supply, Hermann Maurice, Marshal de Saxe, stands out as an original thinker. Although German-born, he won fame fighting for France.

His major battle during the War of the Austrian Succession was at Fontenoy on May 10, 1745. Despite being confined to a stretcher through illness, he took to his horse to lead a decisive counterattack that won the battle for France. He was made a marshal of France by a grateful King Louis XV in 1748. Saxe retired from military service shortly afterward and settled at his country estate. He died there on November 30, 1750.

Saxe's military genius lay in his ability to combine all types of troops, chiefly line infantry, light infantry, artillery, and cavalry, in a single formation. He explained the value of these ideas in his own writings.

Napoleon Bonaparte used these ideas some 50 years later when he introduced the all-arms corps to the French army.

The Marshal of Saxe was a fine commander for the French and was also a noted military thinker.

Rhine to oppose the Austrians there, while the third was ordered to support the Spanish attacks against Austrian-held northern Italy. The Austrians struck first, striking across the Rhine. France's King Louis XV rushed reinforcements south but was taken ill. French operations ceased—for the moment.

Advance on Vienna

The Prussians, alarmed by Austrian successes in 1743, declared war again in August 1744, allying with the French. Moving with lightning speed, Frederick advanced into Bohemia and captured its capital, Prague, in September. He then moved toward Vienna, the Austrian capital. The Austrians, however, were equally rapid

WARFARE IN THE 18TH CENTURY

France's Marshal de Saxe (mounted on the white horse) is surrounded by his troops after his victory at the Battle of Fontenoy in May 1745.

in their response. Newly raised units were rushed to the front to block Frederick's advance and the Austrian army along the Rhine was rushed south.

Frederick recognized the seriousness of the situation. He was isolated in a hostile region and was facing the might of the combined Austrian armies. His French allies were inactive, so there would be no help from them. Frederick fell back into Silesia in November. Encouraged by their success against Frederick, the Austrians invaded Bavaria and took most of it by March.

The English defeated

The Austrians also received good news in January—Austria, Britain, the Netherlands, and Saxony formed an alliance to oppose France, Bavaria, and Prussia. On April 22, 1745, Austria and Bavaria signed a peace treaty. Bavaria gave up all claims to the Austrian throne and Austria returned the captured Bavarian lands. Prussia had lost one of its main allies.

In May the French renewed their war against the multinational force in northern Europe. The French commander, the Marshal de Saxe, hoped to lure the enemy army led by the Duke of Cumberland into open battle by besieging the Flanders city of Tournai. The plan worked and the two rivals met at Fontenoy on May 10. It was a bloody, close-fought battle, with the troops of both sides displaying great valor. The Duke of Cumberland was forced to withdraw in good order. Taking advantage of their victory, the French were able to conquer Flanders by September.

The Battle of Fontenoy

The Battle of Fontenoy, fought on May 10, 1745, was a bloody slogging match between a 52,000-strong French force under the Marshal de Saxe and a 50,000-strong multi-national army led by Britain's Duke of Cumberland. Saxe, though ill, continued to command and positioned his men behind trenches and earthworks, protected by his artillery.

After a failed attack in the morning the Duke of Cumberland launched a massive column of 15,000 men against the French center. The column faced a hail of shot and shell but crashed through the first French line.

Saxe, however, was equal to the challenge. Rising from his sickbed, he organized a second line of defense. French muskets and artillery firing at close range finally halted the huge column in its tracks and cavalry charges forced its survivors to fall back, although slowly.

The failure of the British onslaught against the French center signaled the end of the battle. Cumberland withdrew his army in good order and the French were left in possession of the battlefield. Both sides suffered about 7,500 casualties.

The Battle of Fontenoy was characterized by the unimaginative planning of the Duke of Cumberland, who dispensed with any crafty moves or trickery and simply launched his infantry against the center of the French line. Despite the bravery of his troops, the attack was thrown back by the French.

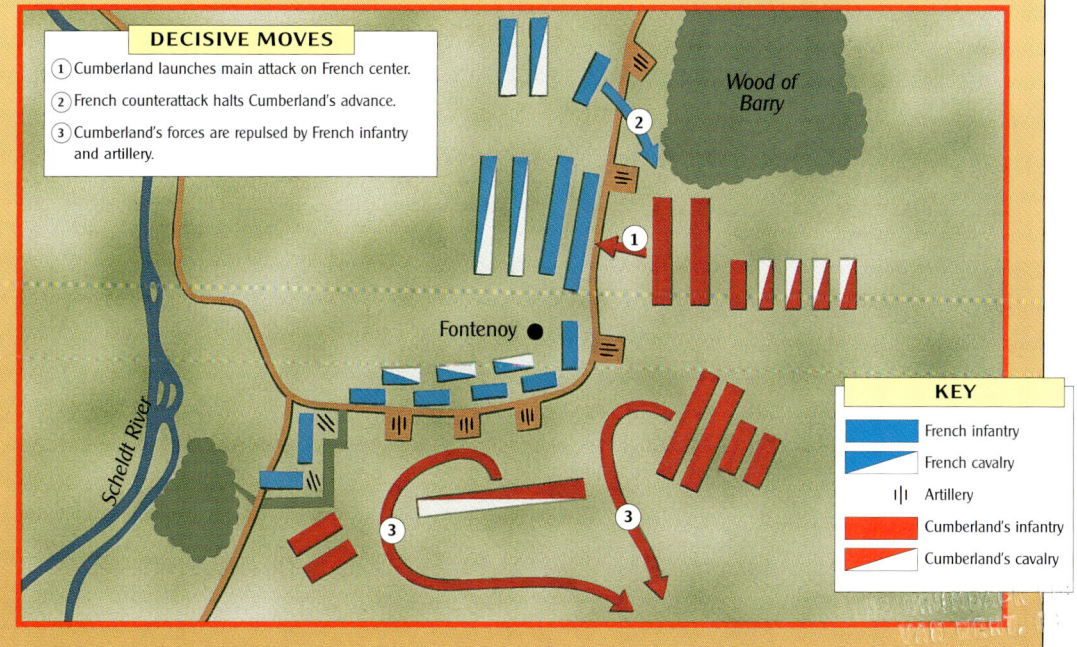

Warfare in the 18th Century

Austria was eager to win back Silesia from the Prussians. However, Frederick lured them into a false sense of security, allowing the Austrians to advance on the town of Breslau. The Austrians camped nearby at Hohenfriedberg, believing that Frederick was still many miles away. Frederick made a rapid night march and by dawn of June 4 his army was ready to fight. Hohenfriedberg was a decisive, one-sided affair. The battle was over by early morning. Caught by surprise, the Austrians had 16,000 casualties. Frederick had barely 1,000.

Prussia invaded

Frederick next advanced into Bohemia. The war degenerated into one of inconclusive maneuver. The Prussian army got smaller and smaller through desertion and illness but the Austrians were unwilling to offer battle after the mauling they had suffered at Hohenfriedberg. Frederick, seeing his army melting away, chose to fall back into Silesia. Seizing their chance, the Austrians made a rapid march, overtook Frederick, and blocked his way at Soor. The battle, on September 30, saw the Prussians punch a way through the Austrians. The road to Silesia was open, but Frederick was still in difficulty.

The Austrians, with vastly superior numbers, invaded Prussia in October. Frederick proved equal to the challenge. In three battles—Katholisch, Hennersdorf, and Görlitz in November—he forced the Austrians back to Bohemia. A second Prussian force

A Prussian regiment advances against the enemy front line during the Battle of Hohenfriedberg on June 4, 1745. The key element in the Prussian victory was the discipline of their infantry. Marching in close ranks, they suffered heavily from enemy fire but were still able to crash through their shaken opponents.

THE WAR OF THE AUSTRIAN SUCCESSION

then defeated an Austrian army at Kesselsdorf on December 14. Maria Theresa, with her will to continue the war dented by Prussia's victories, the French successes in Flanders, and the withdrawal of the British forces in northern Europe, agreed to a peace treaty with Prussia. She recognized Prussia's control of Silesia.

Prussian power

The war was drawing to a close. The French continued operations against Austrian territory in northern Europe throughout 1746 and then invaded the Netherlands in 1747. The war dragged on into May 1748 but peace was now being negotiated.

The Treaty of Aix-la-Chapelle was signed on October 18. Most of the conquered territories were returned to their original owners, although Prussia kept Silesia. The right of Maria Theresa to rule in Austria was agreed. The prewar situation was in effect retained—but with one important difference. Frederick was the head of a Prussian state that was more powerful than ever before. It was a power that Frederick was destined to wield against his European rivals again in the next few years.

The aftermath of Hohenfriedberg, the battle between Frederick the Great's Prussians and an army of Austrians and Saxons. Frederick (mounted on the white horse) salutes his troops as they parade captured flags and prisoners.

31

THE JACOBITE REBELLIONS

Events in the late 17th and early 18th centuries laid the foundations for a string of short wars known as the Jacobite Rebellions. In 1688 Catholic King James II was ousted from the throne of England and fled to France. He was replaced by Protestant King William III. In 1701 the English stated that only Protestants could become monarchs. In 1707, under the Act of Union, England and Scotland were united. Some Scottish Catholics, who were called Jacobites, wanted to put a Catholic back on the throne of the whole kingdom.

James II, a Scot, died in 1701 and James Edward Stuart, James's son, was recognized as the rightful king of England in his place by King Louis XIV of France. James Edward Stuart, known as the "Old Pretender" to the English, tried to regain the throne on two occasions. Awful weather, bad luck, lack of support in Scotland, and the swift response of the English defeated his plans in 1708 and 1715. Despite the help of a small Spanish expeditionary force, a third uprising, in 1719, also failed. The fourth rebellion, in 1745, came much closer to succeeding, however.

The climax of the Battle of Culloden fought on April 16, 1746. The Jacobites charge to destruction against the musket and artillery fire of the government infantry.

The Young Pretender arrives

The son of James Edward Stuart, Charles Edward Stuart, arrived in Scotland—almost alone—in August 1745. Thousands of Scottish Highlanders (members of tribal clans from the mountainous north of Scotland) rallied to his cause. Scotland was poorly garrisoned by the English, who were heavy committed to the War of the Austrian Succession in Europe. Charles, known as the "Young Pretender," captured Edinburgh, the capital of Scotland, and then defeated an English, or government, force a short distance outside Edinburgh at Prestonpans.

Elated by these victories Charles and his army of 5,000 invaded England, intending to rally English Jacobites to their cause and then march on London. The Jacobites reached Derby, less than

250 miles (400 km) from London. Though they did not know it, this was the high tide of the rebellion. Many of Charles's Highlanders were returning home to gather the harvest, promised French support had not arrived, and two government armies were heading north. Charles had to head back to Scotland.

As the rival forces headed north, there were some inconclusive skirmishes and a full-scale battle, at Falkirk in central Scotland on January 17, 1746, which the Jacobites won. However, Charles's army was falling apart. Low morale, war-weariness, and the lack of supplies saw many of his Highlanders desert. Charles planned one last, desperate gamble before his army melted away completely. He decided to launch a night attack on the main government army, which was commanded by the Duke of Cumberland.

Defeat on Culloden Moor

The night attack failed to take place and when dawn broke on April 16 the two armies faced each other across Culloden Moor outside the city of Aberdeen on the northeast coast of Scotland.

The Duke of Cumberland put his artillery to good use in the battle, bombarding the Jacobite line. As their casualties mounted, the Highlanders charged across the boggy moor. The charge was poorly coordinated and was under fire from flank and front for much of the crossing. A few Highlanders actually reached the left of the government front line, breaking through to the second, only to be cut down. The charge lost its momentum, broke on the government bayonets, and the exhausted Highlanders fled. The Young Pretender abandoned his army.

The English moved swiftly to prevent further rebellions in Scotland. Charles was hunted, although he was able to escape back to France. Many of the leading Jacobites were captured, tried, and in most cases executed.

RIVAL TACTICS

The Jacobite Highlanders were not professional soldiers. Their chief tactic was a wild charge. But it was an all-or-nothing tactic. If the charge could be halted, the Highlanders stood little change of winning.

At Culloden the Duke of Cumberland used his artillery to kill Highlanders and provoke the rest into making a charge. As the Highlanders' charge was slowed crossing the boggy moor, many more were cut down by musket volleys.

The duke had also introduced a new tactic for hand-to-hand fighting. A soldier would normally use his bayonet to attack the Highlander to his immediate front. A Highlander was often able to deflect the bayonet thrust with his shield (held on the left arm) and then cut his opponent down with the sword held in his right hand. At Culloden each government soldier attacked the Highlander to his right, thrusting his bayonet into the Highlander's unprotected right side.

Early Native American Wars

Conflict between the Native American population in North America and the European settlers dated back to the arrival of the first settlers in the 17th century. From the mid-18th century the European settlers and colonial governments concentrated on expanding the lands they controlled along the eastern seaboard—at the expense of the Native Americans. The various wars—punctuated by periods of uneasy peace—were brutal. Atrocities and massacres were committed by both colonists and Native Americans.

The interior of North America was virtually unknown to the colonists and few understood the attachment of the Native Americans to their long-standing homelands. Native American culture and way of life were so at odds with those of the colonists that many settlers saw the Native Americans as nothing more than obstacles to be brushed aside with little thought. As the colonialist population along the eastern seaboard grew, settlers headed west eager to exploit and develop new territory. Native Americans, however, were determined to resist the loss of their tribal homelands and preserve their cultures.

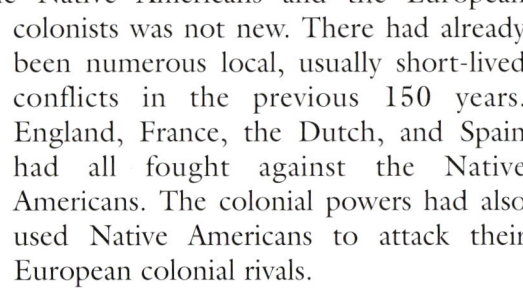

A Native American war party keeps watch over a colonial farmstead. Both colonists and Native Americans launched periodic attacks on isolated farms and small settlements.

Long-standing conflict

Friction between the Native Americans and the European colonists was not new. There had already been numerous local, usually short-lived conflicts in the previous 150 years. England, France, the Dutch, and Spain had all fought against the Native Americans. The colonial powers had also used Native Americans to attack their European colonial rivals.

The 17th century saw many small-scale wars between the Native Americans, the great European powers, and their settlers. On paper at least the Native Americans had many advantages—there were more of them and they were skilled fighters. The colonists lived in small, widely scattered homesteads or small settlements, and the

KING PHILIP'S WAR

In June 1675, the leader of the Wampanoag, Philip (his tribal name was Metacomet), launched a series of attacks against European colonial settlements in southern New England. Philip objected to the steady movement of the European colonists into his tribal homelands and the conversion of many of his tribespeople to the Christian faith.

When Philip's brother, Alexander (Wamsutta), complained to the colonial authorities, he was imprisoned and then died shortly after his release. Philip went to war with the settlers.

A dozen English settlements, most in what is now Massachusetts, were destroyed before the New England Confederation declared war on Philip.

Philip, however, was betrayed by one of his own tribespeople and suffered a major defeat at the Great Swamp Fight in Rhode Island. Philip was killed at Mount Hope in August 1676 after the position of his hideaway had been revealed to the colonists by one of the chief's own people.

After Philip's death his head was cut off by the colonists and displayed on a pole at Plymouth, a warning to any Native Americans contemplating rising up against the colonists.

The war ended in southern New England in 1676, but dragged on in northern New England until 1678. The colonists had 500 settlers killed or captured. Between 12 and 20 colonial settlements were abandoned or destroyed.

leading European colonial powers were generally unwilling to send anything more than token regular forces to protect their distant colonies in North America.

Local defense forces

By and large the colonies had to provide for their own defense. They relied on militias formed from able-bodied colonists of military age. However, these were civilians in arms and not trained soldiers. Most would fight to protect their own farms or those of their neighbors, but they were unwilling to travel far or campaign against the Native Americans for long. Many had to return home to bring in the harvest. Those who ran the colonies were also often reluctant to go to the aid of another colony.

The colonists, at first glance, seemed ill-prepared to take on the Native Americans. However, the Native Americans were far from united in their dealings with the colonists. Tribes often sided with the colonists if the colonists were fighting one of their traditional Native American enemies.

Native Americans often found it difficult to present a united front against the colonists. When Native Americans did win a battle or skirmish, they often failed to take advantage of their success. A single victory in a war against another North American tribe often decided the outcome of the war. This was not the case when the Native Americans took on the colonists.

Pontiac's uprising

One of the greatest threats to British control of North America right after the Seven Years War, the French and Indian War, (see pages 38–47) in the middle of the 18th century was led by Pontiac, a chief of the Ottawa. Pontiac had supported the French during the fighting between 1756 and 1763. When the French were on the point of being evicted from North America near the end of the war, the British allowed settlers to move into areas previously occupied by the French. These settlers took over Native American land, and the British did nothing to stop them.

Pontiac was outraged by the turn of events and was able to unite many of the Native American tribes against the British in 1762. These recruits from other tribes gave Pontiac about 900 warriors to take on the British and colonists. When the fighting began the following year, Pontiac decided to attack as many British forts as possible. He saw that the British forces in North America were spread thinly. If he attacked at several points, the scattered British garrisons would not be able to unite against him.

Pontiac's warriors keep a close watch on Fort Detroit during the siege that lasted until Pontiac was forced to retreat due to defeats elsewhere.

EARLY NATIVE AMERICAN WARS

The major battles of King Philip's War in the 1670s and Pontiac's uprising in the 1760s. The Native Americans were defeated in both, allowing European colonists to move farther west into the interior of North America.

Pontiac's plans went well. On May 7, 1763, he led a surprise attack on Detroit, one of the few forts still held by the British. Pontiac's plans were, in fact, known to the British, who defeated the surprise attack. Rather than retreat, Pontiac decided to besiege the fort. When the defenders of Detroit charged out from their fort to attack Pontiac's forces in late July, they were defeated at the Battle of Bloody Ridge. The siege continued until October, but other events were about to end the uprising.

Forced to retreat

In the first week of August a British relief column led by Colonel Henry Bouquet was ambushed by Pontiac's men. Bouquet, however, placed his supply wagons in a circle to protect his men. The Native Americans attacked but Bouquet defeated them.

This fight, the Battle of Bushy Run, was decisive. Bouquet was able to relieve one of the other British forces under siege, leaving Pontiac no choice but to give up the siege of Detroit. The Native American alliance fell apart after the defeat at Bushy Run. Pontiac and a handful of his diehard supporters tried to forge a new anti-British alliance but failed. Pontiac agreed to a truce in 1765 and a permanent peace treaty was signed on July 25, 1766. Pontiac was killed by another Native American in 1769.

Native Americans continued to fight against European settlers until the end of the 19th century. The pattern of Native American territorial loss established in the 17th and 18th centuries, however, was repeated over and over.

NORTH AMERICA'S ANGLO–FRENCH WARS

By the middle of the 18th century both France and Britain were busy expanding their spheres of influence in North America. These bitter rivals had already fought each other in North America from 1744 to 1748, during King George's War, the name given to the part of the War of the Austrian Succession fought in North America. The French and British went to war again from 1754 to 1763. This second conflict, known as the French and Indian War, decided which of the two powers would control the continent.

The French controlled an area of North America stretching southwest from the northeast coast down the St. Lawrence River, the area around the Great Lakes, and a huge territory, known then as Louisiana, that stretched westward from the Great Lakes to the Rockies and south to the coast of the Gulf of Mexico. The British held most of the eastern seaboard.

French hunters and backwoodsmen had been heading down the valley of the Ohio River from Canada for many years, suggesting that full-scale settlement in an area that the British and their North American colonists saw as rightfully theirs might soon take place. To reinforce the British claim, Governor Robert Dinwiddie ordered a young officer, Colonel George Washington, and a band of Virginia militia to build a fort in early 1754 where the Allegheny and Monongahela Rivers meet (now the site of Pittsburgh).

George Washington was a militia colonel fighting for the British during the wars against the French.

Surrender to the French

However, Washington's plans were spoiled by the French, who had already built a stockade—Fort Duquesne—at the junction of the rivers. Washington pulled back and built Fort Necessity at nearby Great Meadows. The fort was only partly finished when the French attacked. Washington and his militia put up some resistance but were eventually forced to surrender to the French. The militiamen were granted the full honors of war and allowed to leave with their weapons.

Both the French and British began to send fresh troops to North America. First to arrive, in the spring of 1755, was General Edward Braddock with two British regiments. After a meeting with colonial leaders it was agreed that four separate attacks should be made against the French. Braddock was to lead a force of 1,500 British troops and 450 colonial militiamen against Fort Duquesne. It was a difficult journey through dense, dark forest along little more than tracks. The column, burdened down with all the heavy equipment of an army going to war in Europe, made slow progress.

Ambush in the forest

If Braddock was expecting to meet the French in an open, European-style battle, with his regulars exchanging close-range musket volleys with the French, he was much mistaken. The French and their Native American allies, no more than 900 men in total, ambushed the British as they were trudging through the dense forest after crossing over the Monongahela River. The French and Native Americans, firing from cover behind trees, bushes, and fallen branches, destroyed a large part of the front and flanks of the column as the British attempted to carry out precision parade-ground maneuvers in the tangled undergrowth.

Panic set in. Many of the British attempted to flee, leaving small groups of their comrades to hold off the French as they closed in for the kill. Braddock was shot down and died from his wounds. Washington, a volunteer with the column, managed to organize a rearguard and lead some of the column to safety.

There was, however, no disguising the seriousness of the defeat. The only sizeable British force in the region had been annihilated—over half of Braddock's men were killed. The French and their Native American allies were free to roam up and down the Ohio River valley, attacking isolated farmsteads and settlements at will.

British and American soldiers rush to the aid of the mortally wounded General Edward Braddock at the Battle of Monongahela on July 9, 1755.

39

Warfare in the 18th Century

The next expedition to attempt to halt French expansion south from Canada was a local affair. General William Johnson was sent from Albany toward Crown Point at the head of 3,500 colonial militiamen and a few hundred Native Americans. A French force of 2,000 regulars, French-Canadian militiamen, and Native Americans advanced to block Johnson's column.

The war intensifies

The two forces blundered into each other at the head of Lake George and the September 8, 1755, battle was a decisive victory for Johnson. The French commander, Ludwig Dieskau, was captured. Johnson, however was unable to use his advantage. His militia refused to continue—as they had the right to do. Johnson decided to build a stockade, Fort William Henry, and station a few troops there. The French fell back to Ticonderoga.

The fact that the war was falling into a deadlock was confirmed by the fate of an expedition against French-held Fort Niagara by Governor William Shirley of Massachusetts between August and September 1755. Shirley marched up the Mohawk River valley with 1,500 troops only to return to Albany when faced with the prospect of taking on French regulars. However, the conflict in North America was about to intensify. The Seven Years War began in Europe in 1756. Britain and France, enemies

A contemporary view of the Battle of Lake George on September 8, 1755. A force of American militia and Native Americans (seen here at right) defeated a mixed force of 2,000 French regulars, French-Canadians, and Native Americans.

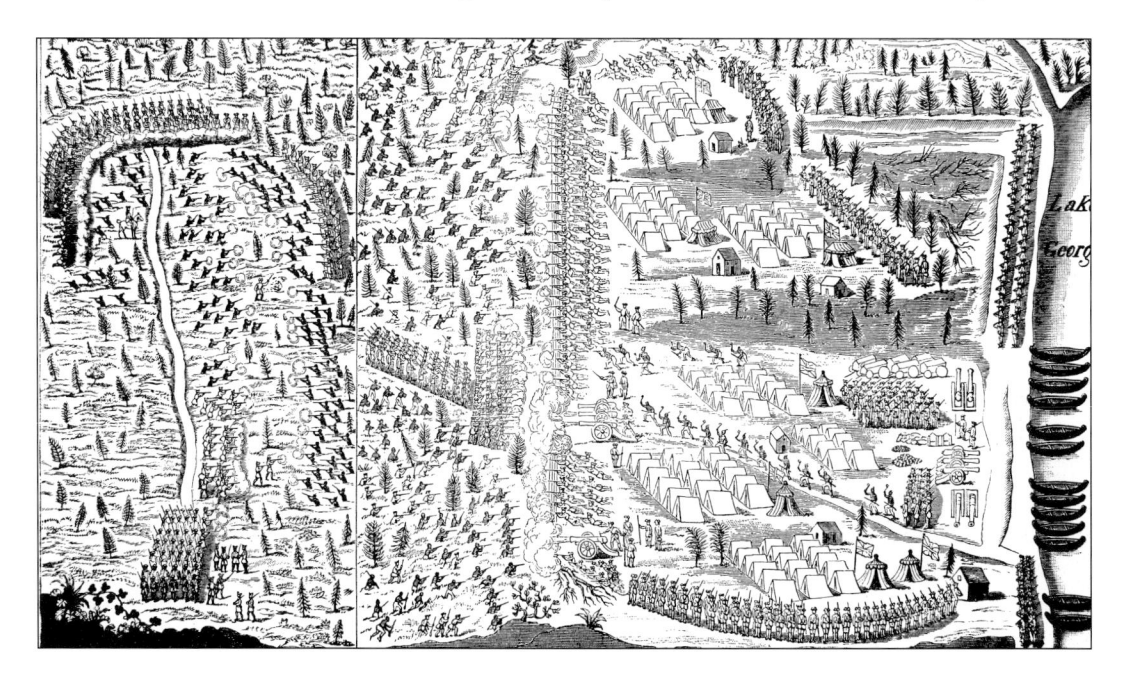

NORTH AMERICA'S ANGLO-FRENCH WARS

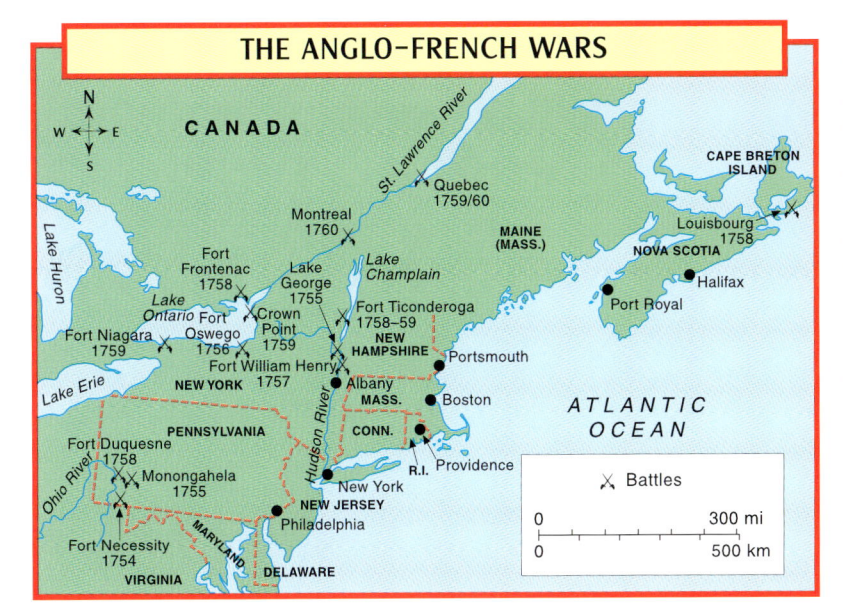

The campaigns that were fought during the Anglo-French Wars were influenced by geography. Roads were few in the interior and waterways were the main routes used by the rival European forces and their local allies.

in the Seven Years War, rushed troops to North America, each fearing that the other would make more determined efforts to take over its colonies.

Two rival generals arrived—France's Marquis Louis Joseph de Montcalm in May and Britain's Lord Loudoun in July. Montcalm was first off the mark. In August he crossed Lake Ontario. He made a lightning attack against Oswego, which he destroyed, and then settled down at Ticonderoga. Loudoun did not intervene, and both sides went into their winter quarters.

When spring 1758 brought better weather, Loudoun was ordered to take part in an amphibious (land and water) operation against Louisbourg, a vital French fort in Nova Scotia. However, the French reinforced their garrison in the fort and sailed a fleet into the harbor. When a British fleet was scattered by a storm, the expedition was canceled. Loudoun returned to New York.

Massacre at Fort William Henry

With the bulk of the British forces in North America involved in the Louisbourg expedition, the frontier was desperately short of troops to stop any French attack. Montcalm took advantage of this and laid siege to Fort William Henry. Heavily outnumbered by Montcalm's 5,000 regulars, militia, and Native Americans, the British garrison put up a brave defense but the fort could not withstand the pounding dished out by the French siege artillery.

41

Irregular Warfare

While there were regular European troops deployed in the war, they were not trained to act or think as individuals. Their role was to stand in tightly packed ranks and exchange close-range volley fire with the enemy. Traditional battles, therefore required flat, open terrain where such a tactic could be used. However, such battles were rare in the dense forests and rugged uplands of North America.

Both sides, the French initially more so, used local forces, colonial militias, volunteers, and Native Americans to wage a guerrilla-type war of swift marches, ambushes from cover, and attacks on the enemy's weak and isolated garrisons.

These troops were tough frontiersmen, men with the skills needed to live off the land and move stealthily through the forest. Most, being hunters, were excellent shots. The British did not make the best use of such men at least at first, believing their colonial troops were too wild and poorly disciplined to be of much use. However, when they recognized their value, various regiments and corps were raised from the backwoodsmen. One of the most famous was Rogers' Rangers.

Members of Rogers' Rangers on patrol along the disputed frontier in the depths of winter. These hardy, skilled backswoodsmen fought for the British and became experts at guerrilla warfare.

The fort's commander sought surrender terms. Montcalm, a gracious commander, was impressed by the British defense and granted terms. The garrison would be allowed to leave with its weapons and flags on condition that its members agreed not to take part in further fighting. The terms were agreed.

The events that followed remain controversial. The British garrison marched out of Fort William Henry on August 9, 1757, to make its way to Albany. It never reached safety. Once outside the fort the column was ambushed by Montcalm's Native

American allies. Many of the garrison were massacred, including most of the women, and children. Montcalm destroyed Fort William Henry and took his army into winter quarters.

The British stung by the massacre at Fort William Henry prepared to redouble their efforts to end French involvement in North America. Under the dynamic leadership of a new prime minister, William Pitt, a new two-pronged strategy was devised. Loudoun was replaced by General James Abercrombie, who was ordered to strike at Ticonderoga and Duquesne. General Jeffrey Amherst was given the task of attacking Louisbourg. Montcalm would not be able to deal with both threats at the same time.

Disaster at Ticonderoga

Amherst's expedition against Louisbourg began in May 1758. The fortress was surrounded by Amherst's force of 9,000 British regulars and 500 colonial militiamen. Louisbourg was a tough nut to crack and both sides displayed great resourcefulness in the siege. However, the fortress was forced to surrender on July 27. One of the British officers, General James Wolfe, was singled out for praise. The capture of Louisbourg, the main French base in Canada, was a British success, but it was balanced by a disaster.

While Amherst was attacking Louisbourg, Abercrombie was fulfilling his role in the two-pronged strategy—but with little success. He foolishly launched an all-out frontal assault against the French position guarding the main route to Ticonderoga on July 8. Abercrombie had 12,000 men, half British regulars, under his

British troops try to storm the French defenses outside Fort Ticonderoga on July 8, 1758. The French won a resounding victory.

command; Montcalm about 3,000. Montcalm placed his men behind a ditch protected by felled, sharpened branches and a wooden fence. Safe behind these barriers his troops shot the British attack to pieces. Abercrombie lost 1,500 casualties—and later his job—for his part in the disaster at Ticonderoga.

French defeats

The French, however, suffered two setbacks in the second half of 1758. They were forced to abandon Fort Duquesne in November when confronted by a column led by General John Forbes. A force of colonial militia under Colonel John Bradstreet also captured Fort Frontenac on Lake Ontario.

At both Fort Duquesne and Fort Frontenac American colonial forces played a major role in deciding the outcome of the fighting. They displayed the flexibility and specialist fighting skills often found lacking in the regular regiments of the British army. These backwoodsmen, top marksmen and skilled in fieldcraft, could take on the French-Canadian militias and Native Americans on their own terms.

In 1759, the decisive year of the war, the British launched a three-pronged offensive against the French. The targets were Fort Niagara, Fort Ticonderoga, and Quebec. Some 2,000 British troops under General John Prideaux captured Fort Niagara on July 25, although Prideaux was killed. A large mixed force of colonial and British troops under Amherst took Ticonderoga the next day and then captured Crown Point. However, the decisive battle was for Quebec.

The decisive battle

The British under General James Wolfe landed just below Quebec on June 26. They faced a large French force under Montcalm that was amply supplied with artillery and held a city with massive protecting walls sited high above the St. Lawrence River. The British would find it very difficult to storm the city's walls and casualties were likely to be very heavy.

Wolfe spent two fruitless months trying to get his men into a position from where they could attack Quebec. Wolfe and his generals faced the possibility of abandoning the campaign if they did not act quickly. Winter was approaching and Wolfe's naval support was preparing to leave the St. Lawrence to avoid being frozen in. Just as it seemed that the attack would have to be canceled, a narrow track was found that led up the steep cliffs to the

MARQUIS DE MONTCALM

Born into an aristocratic French family in 1712, Montcalm was a military man through and through. He began his career at the age of 12 and saw extensive service in European wars in the 1730s and 1740s. He gained rapid promotion and was appointed to command in Canada in January 1756.

Montcalm was a charming man and popular with his troops. However, his position in Canada was delicate and difficult. When he arrived, Montcalm discovered that he had no control over the local militias and colonial troops. These valuable additions to his meager supply of regulars were handled by the French governor, the Marquis de Vaudreuil. Relations between the two men were always strained, even after Montcalm was given authority over the governor.

The friction between Montcalm and the governor played a role in the defeat at Quebec in 1759 (see pages 46–47). Montcalm had more troops than the British and there was a plentiful supply of artillery in the city. However, Vaudreuil refused to release the artillery or militias. When Montcalm and his French regulars marched out onto the Plains of Abraham, above Quebec, they were lacking the cannon that might have brought them victory.

Montcalm (center) acknowledges the cheers of his troops after their victory over the British outside Ticonderoga in 1758.

west of Quebec. The track led to a flat, open area of ground, the Plains of Abraham, just outside the walls of Quebec—an ideal spot for a conventional battle.

On the night of September 12 Wolfe and his men landed and scaled the steep cliffs without being spotted by the French sentries. When morning dawned on the 13th, the mixed British and colonial force of about 5,000 men deployed for battle on the Plains of Abraham. Montcalm realized that he had no option but to leave the protection of the city and offer battle to the British, otherwise his supply lines would be cut. His forces would then be starved into surrender.

Warfare in the 18th Century

The French, some 4,500 men, marched across the Plains of Abraham to meet the British. Few shots were fired until the French were very close to the British. Then a single volley rang out from the ranks of the British troops. When the smoke cleared, the French attack was over, hundreds of Montcalm's soldiers had been either killed or wounded. The rest fled back into Quebec. Wolfe never enjoyed his victory, however. Both he and Montcalm died from battle wounds. Wolfe died on the same day as the battle, while Montcalm survived until the next day.

Britain takes over Canada

The French made one unsuccessful attempt to recapture Quebec in the spring of 1760. But after losing their main commander and field army at Quebec, and then faced with three British columns marching against Montreal, defeat was certain. On September 8, 1760, the French governor, the Marquis de Vaudreuil, surrendered to the British, ending his country's control of Canada. Britain's domination of Canada was confirmed by the terms of the Treaty of Paris in February 1763. The single volley fired by Wolfe's troops outside Quebec on September 13, 1759, had settled the fate of Canada.

The Battle of Quebec, fought between the French and British on September 13, 1759, confirmed that Britain would be the major power in colonial North America. This late 18th-century picture shows British troops scaling the cliffs and then using volley fire to destroy a large part of the French forces.

THE BATTLE OF QUEBEC

James Wolfe was the son of a British officer. Although he was determined to follow in his father's footsteps, he was plagued by poor health as a boy. Nevertheless, he entered the army in 1741 at the age of 14. Wolfe saw service in northern Europe and played a distinguished role in the defeat of the 1745 Jacobite rebellion in Scotland.

Wolfe was not always popular with other senior officers, who made public criticisms of him. However, Wolfe enjoyed the confidence of King George II. The king once dismissed criticism of Wolfe by saying: "Mad is he? Then I hope he will bite some other of my generals."

Wolfe was sent to Canada in 1758, and took part in the attack on Louisbourg. After a brief spell back in England he was given command of the British expedition against Quebec.

Quebec was very difficult to attack and the British came close to abandoning all hope of taking the city. But Wolfe took a gamble to land his forces upstream and then take on the French. The plan worked but Wolfe was mortally injured. He died on September 13, 1759, the day he won the battle that decided the fate of Canada.

The French defenses around Quebec were very extensive and the British had great difficulty in getting close enough to the city to place it under siege. Wolfe's daring plan to put troops on the Plains of Abraham forced the French to fight in the open.

DECISIVE MOVES

1. British move to new camp on June 9.
2. Wolfe moves troops by flat-bottomed boats on September 12.
3. British troops scale cliffs during the night of September 12.
4. French attack defeated on the Plains of Abraham on morning of September 13.

KEY

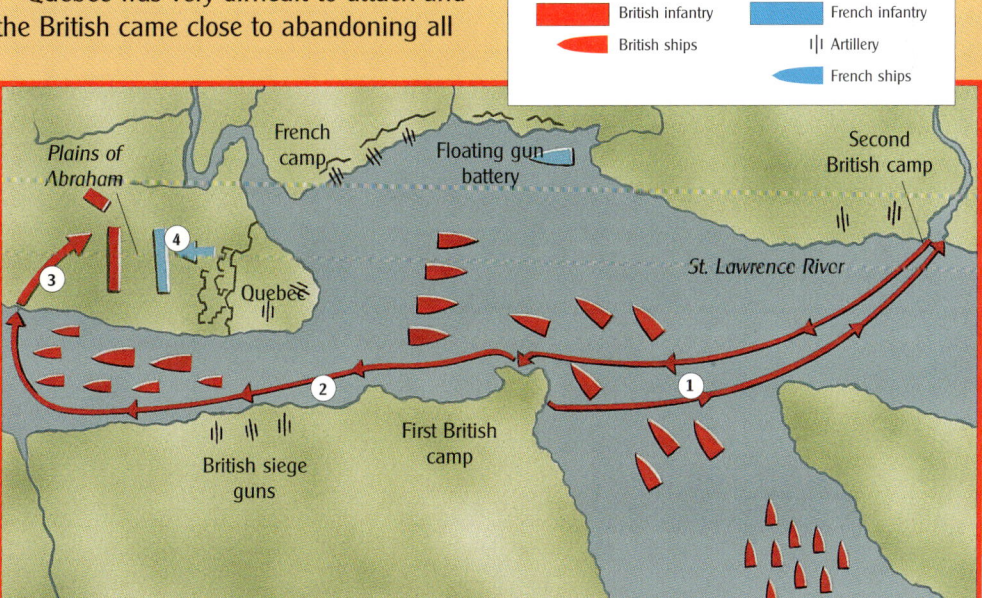

- British infantry
- British ships
- French infantry
- Artillery
- French ships

Europe's Struggle for India

By the mid-18th century India, a country split between many large and small kingdoms, was in turmoil. The once dominant Mughal Empire was falling apart under pressure from the north, where invaders had seized the area of what is now Afghanistan and were pressing southward into Mughal lands. From the south the Maratha people were pushing north. India was also the target of European powers eager to grab valuable colonies. Chief among these were Britain and France, already deadly foes in Europe.

Robert Clive, the man whose victory at the Battle of Plassey in 1757 made sure that the British, not the French, would be the dominant power in Indian political affairs.

For much of the first half of the 18th century Britain and France were content to established bases along the coastline of India, from where they traded with local rulers. Both countries created practically independent organizations to oversee their trade with India—the British East India Company and the French East India Company. These two bodies, who also acted as their countries political representatives in India, were rivals. Both used local Indian warlords and princes to their own advantage. Both of the companies had their own armies, but also received support from their countries' regular armed forces. Both companies were cover organizations for their respective governments and were, in reality, virtually the same thing. They did, however, very much run their own affairs in India.

The first battles

The first clashes between the two were provoked by the outbreak of the War of the Austrian Succession in Europe in 1744. The French, led by Marquis Joseph Dupleix, captured the main British base, Madras, in 1746 and then tried to capture Fort St. George. The siege lasted some 18 months. The timely arrival of British reinforcements under Admiral Edward Boscawen saved St. George, and Boscawen then tried—unsuccessfully—to capture the main French base at Pondicherry in 1748. This first war in India between France and Britain ended in stalemate the same year.

The two rival companies, although supposedly at peace, used local conflicts to further their ambitions. In 1749 French troops sided with a number of warlords rebelling against a group of legitimate rulers. The British, in contrast, aided the established rulers. A combined French-Indian force won the Battle of Ambur and killed Anwar-ud-din, one of the established rulers. Anwar-ud-din was replaced by Chanda Sahib, but real power was exercised by Dupleix. With the backing of the British East India Company, one of the remaining legitimate rulers, Nasir Jang, tried to win back the lands lost due to the Battle of Ambur.

France gains territory

Nasir Jang was partly successful, but was assassinated by his son, Muzaffar Jang, who promptly seized power in December 1750. Dupleix supported Muzaffar Jang. In return for the support of the French forces in India the new ruler gave Dupleix control of a large expanse of former Mughal lands. For the moment the British seemed powerless to prevent the French extending their control over India. Dupleix, with local support, ruled over a great area of southern India, while the commander of his small French army, General Charles Bussy-Castelnau, was active in the center of the country.

In the second half of 1751, however, British fortunes in India underwent a remarkable revival. Much of this was due to the fighting spirit of one person—Robert Clive. Clive was not a man with a long military history. He had, in fact, been a lowly official in the East India Company. His chance came when an Indian army allied to the French laid siege to the British at Trichinopoly.

Clive's first battle

Clive gathered together just 500 troops and three cannon at Madras, but rather than march directly to the relief of Trichinopoly, he captured the capital of the Indian ruler besieging the town. The ruler's son, Raja Sahib, was immediately sent to this capital, Arcot, with 10,000 men and in turn laid siege to Clive's force. The siege dragged on for over 50 days. Battle casualties, disease, and hunger reduced Clive's already tiny force further until he had only 120 European soldiers and 250 sepoys (native Indian troops fighting for the British) left.

WARFARE IN THE 18TH CENTURY

> ## ROBERT CLIVE
>
> Robert Clive had no military training and began his career with the British East India Company when he was sent to the port city of Madras, India, in the fall of 1743. He was employed as a clerk and appears not to have been very successful in this position. Clive's military career in India began when he volunteered for service in the army and was made a junior officer in 1748.
>
> His great chance came in 1751, when he played the key role in the defense of Arcot. After a spell back in Britain he returned to India in June 1756 and took part in an unbroken run of victories. He captured Calcutta in January 1757, took the French-held port of Chandernagore in March, and won a great victory at Plassey in June. In a year he had transformed Britain's position in India. Because of his victories India was destined to become part of a British and not a French empire.
>
> There is little doubt that Clive was a "natural" at warfare. He was courageous even in the face of overwhelmingly superior enemy forces and knew how to deal with the various Indian rulers to both his and the British East India Company's advantage. Clive entered politics but his career suffered due to his possibly corrupt dealings. His health declined and he committed suicide in 1774.

Sensing that the British were close to collapse, the Indians launched an all-or-nothing assault against the defenses. A herd of elephants, their heads protected by metal shields, was launched at the city gates to batter them down. Clive knew that wounded elephants were likely to panic so he ordered his weary men to fire on them. The elephants scattered, trampling many of the besiegers. A second Indian assault directed across a moat was beaten back at the point of bayonets. After a little more than an hour the battle was over. Clive had won a great victory.

Attacks on the British

Clive's successful defense of Arcot was more than just a brilliant feat of arms. It also had an important impact on the future of India. France's Indian allies began to loose faith in its ability to run the country to their advantage. Dupleix, although in no way responsible for the Arcot defeat, was dismissed in 1754.

With the French in temporary disorder the British position in India seemed securer that ever. However, powerful Indian warlords and princes made their own attempts to undermine the authority of the British East India Company. In June 1756 the ruler of Bengal, Suraja Dowla, attacked Calcutta, the center of British activity in the country. After a four-day siege the Bengalis took the city. In an act that was destined to strengthen British determination, Suraja Dowla ordered that 146 Europeans his troops had captured were to be placed in a tiny cell. Most perished through lack of water and heat exhaustion. This event, known to the British as the "Black Hole of Calcutta," acted as a rallying call to the British troops in India.

Clive's great victory

The British moved swiftly to stabilize the situation. Clive was sent from Madras to Calcutta and recaptured the city on January 2, 1757. His next task was the capture of the French base at Chandernagore. This was accomplished in March. With his lines of communication to Calcutta secure, Clive could now hunt down Suraja Dowla.

Clive and his small force caught up with the Bengalis in June. On the 23rd Clive's force took on the 50,000-strong Bengali army at Plassey. In one of the most remarkably one-sided battles in history Clive took the fight to the vastly superior Bengali force and crushed it. Clive's victory was so complete that it virtually ended Bengali resistance to the British. It also undermined the

A British view of the "Black Hole of Calcutta," the cell in which the majority of the 146 Europeans thrown into the prison died from heat and lack of water.

WARFARE IN THE 18TH CENTURY

prestige of the French in India as they had never won such a great battle. Suraja Dowla did not survive the defeat for long—he was assassinated a few days later. His replacement, Mir Jafar, became an ally of the British. Bengal was now firmly within the British sphere of influence in India.

The French sent reinforcements to India under General Thomas Lally, an Irishman fighting for his adopted country, in 1758. Lally moved quickly. He left Pondicherry and marched south against the British base of Fort St. David. This fell on June 2 and Lally turned his attention to Madras. The town survived the siege chiefly due to supplies brought in by ship. A British relief force inflicted a sharp reverse on Lally at the Battle of Masulipatam on January 25, 1759.

The fall of Pondicherry

The British decided to keep the pressure on the French. Lally was defeated at the Battle of Wandiwash on January 22, 1760, by General Eyre Coote. The French retreated to their base at Pondicherry, which the British placed under siege in August. The siege dragged on for several months, but events at sea eventually forced Lally to surrender. On September 10, a French naval force of 11 warships under Commodore Anne Antoine d'Ache was battered into defeat by a British squadron led by Admiral George Pocock.

Robert Clive (mounted on the white horse) leads his Anglo-Indian troops to victory at the Battle of Plassey, June 23, 1757.

Britain takes charge

This defeat effectively ended France's hopes of holding its possessions in India. Without supplies or reinforcements reaching Pondicherry, it was only a matter of time before Lally would have to surrender to the British. On January 15, 1761, Lally raised the white flag of surrender over Pondicherry. The French East India Company was closed down in 1769.

The Battle of Plassey

The Battle of Plassey was a triumph for the British and laid the foundations for Britain's domination of the whole of India.

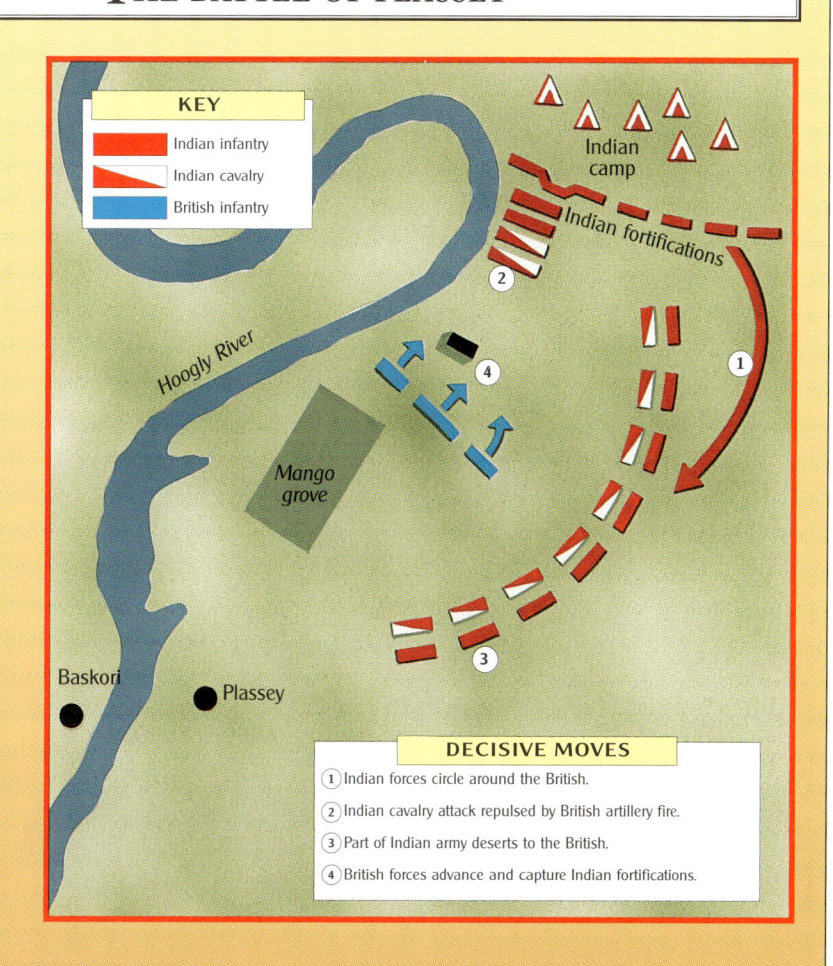

KEY
- Indian infantry
- Indian cavalry
- British infantry

Indian camp
Indian fortifications
Hoogly River
Mango grove
Baskori
Plassey

DECISIVE MOVES
1. Indian forces circle around the British.
2. Indian cavalry attack repulsed by British artillery fire.
3. Part of Indian army deserts to the British.
4. British forces advance and capture Indian fortifications.

If numbers alone are the key to victory then the British should have been absolutely destroyed at Plassey on June 23, 1757. The Indian forces of Suraja Dowla numbered 50,000 men, with more than 50 cannon. Robert Clive had just 1,100 British and 2,100 Indian troops and ten cannon.

However, Clive was an aggressive commander and his small force was disciplined and well-trained. In contrast Suraja Dowla's army was badly armed, poorly led, and lacked training.

All generals need luck. Clive was fortunate that a sudden rainstorm damped the enemy gunpowder. His men kept their powder dry. An Indian cavalry attack was beaten off and Clive then advanced his artillery closer to the enemy fortifications. After bombarding the Indian positions, Clive ordered a bayonet charge. The wavering enemy force collapsed.

Warfare in the 18th Century

With the French out of the way the British moved to extend their influence by taking advantage of the rivalries between various Indian rulers. The British were playing a risky game. Their Indian allies usually expected something in return for supporting the British. When the British failed to support Haidar Ali, the ruler of Mysore (Karnataka), against the Maratha, a people of west-central India, he turned on his supposed allies.

More British victories

In September 1780 Haidar Ali smashed a small British force and then advanced on Madras. General Coote at the head of 8,000 men took on and crushed Haidar Ali's 60,000 troops at the Battle of Porto Novo on June 1, 1781.

This first British success was followed by two more victories in August and September. French support, particularly the capture of the British base of Trincomalee in Ceylon (now Sri Lanka) in August 1782, kept the war going for a time. Much of France's efforts rested on the shoulders of Admiral Pierre André de Suffren, an exceptional naval commander. But the death of Haidar Ali, the ending of French support, and the crowning of a new Mysore ruler, Tippoo Sahib, who favored peace brought the conflict to an end in 1783.

General Sir Eyre Coote leads his outnumbered Anglo-Indian army to victory over Haidar Ali's forces at the Battle of Porto Novo on June 1, 1781.

A ruler bent on revenge

Tippoo Sahib, however, still angered by Mysore's humiliation, sought revenge in 1789. He attacked Travancore, a move that provoked the British to invade Mysore. The British commander, Lord Cornwallis, captured Bangalore and then laid siege to Seringapatam, where Tippoo Sahib had sought refuge. The war ended in 1792. The victorious British gained half of Mysore.

In 1799 the British moved to deal with the remaining French possessions in India. The governor of Britain's colonies in India, Richard Wellesley, ordered Tippoo Sahib to disband the French units under his command. This was done but the Mysore ruler continued to work closely with the French. The British used this as a reason to invade in 1799, laying siege to Seringapatam for the second time. The fighting was bloody but the British captured the city. Tippoo Sahib died defending the city's walls, with his sword in his hand. Richard Wellesley's younger brother, Arthur, who had fought with distinction in the battle, was made governor of Seringapatam.

Arthur Wellesley laid the foundations of a brilliant military career extending British control across India. His victory at Assaye in 1803, when his 5,000 troops defeated a 50,000-strong French-Indian army, confirmed his great promise as a general. His greatest test would come a few years later, when, as the Duke of Wellington, he was destined to take on the might of Napoleonic France in Europe.

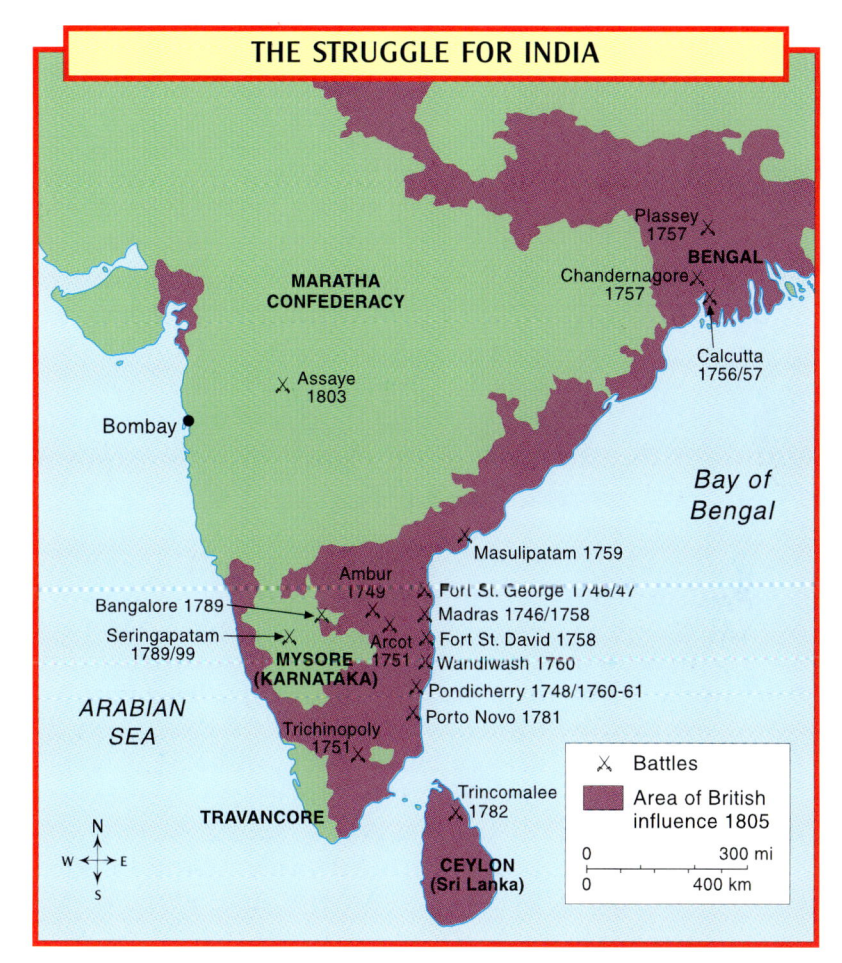

THE STRUGGLE FOR INDIA

The struggle between France and Britain for control of India during the late 18th and early 19th centuries. The French were finally defeated and the British then set about taking control of the whole of the subcontinent.

THE SEVEN YEARS WAR

By the middle of the 18th century it was clear to most European powers that Frederick II of Prussia, known today as Frederick the Great, was determined to carve out an empire in central Europe. In 1756 several other countries—Austria, France, Russia, Sweden, and Saxony—united to stop Frederick. The British were at war with France in North America and India, and sided with the Prussians. The conflict that followed became known as the Seven Years War and was fought mainly in central Europe.

Frederick the Great, king of Prussia from 1740 until his death in 1786, was a dynamic, warlike monarch.

Frederick the Great was an outstanding general, undoubtedly one of the greatest of all time. He saw that he faced, with few allies, most of Europe's great powers. If they combined there was no way his troops could defeat them. He decided to attack first, before his enemies were fully mobilized for war.

Saxony surrenders

Saxony, one of the weaker partners in the enemy alliance, was the target. On August 29, 1756, Frederick invaded at the head of 70,000 men. He took the Saxon capital, Dresden, on September 10 and then marched against a force of Austrians that was moving to help the Saxons. The two armies met at Lobositz on October 1. The Austrians were defeated and the Saxons surrendered. Saxony was Frederick's and its army became part of his own.

Frederick now moved against Austria, invading Bohemia in April 1757. Leaving forces to guard his borders closest to France, Sweden, and Russia, Frederick led 65,000 men against the Austrian army near Prague. The Austrians were beaten on May 6, and the defeated Austrian army retreated into Prague. Prague was besieged. Frederick now took a part of his army, some 32,000 men, to block the approach of an Austrian relief army. He

THE SEVEN YEARS WAR

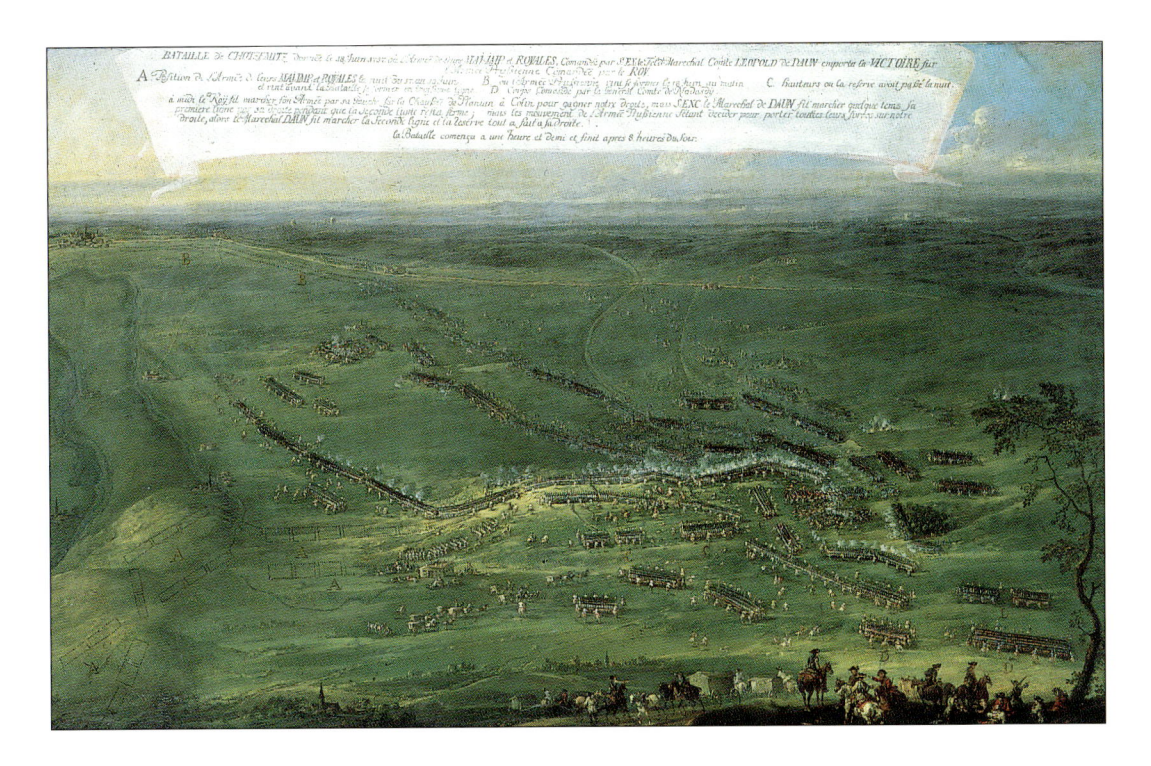

fought the 60,000 Austrians at Kolin on June 18, and came off worst. Frederick suffered 13,500 casualties, abandoned the siege of Prague, and retreated from Bohemia. Frederick now had to deal with threats from all directions.

Prussia under attack

One French army, 100,000-strong, invaded the state of Hanover, while a joint Austro-French army pushed across the central Rhine River. A third army, 100,000-strong, was moving from Bohemia into southern Prussia. Some 100,000 Russians were attacking eastern Prussia, and a Swedish army of 16,000 was driving south from the Baltic Sea. These forces won two victories. On July 26, 1757, Frederick's British allies were defeated at Hastenbeck in Hanover by the French. The Russians defeated a Prussian force at Gross-Jägersdorf on July 30. Austrian forces also attacked the Prussian capital, Berlin, in October.

Frederick was in trouble but kept a cool head. He was aided by the fact that his enemies were slow in following up their successes. After much marching and countermarching Frederick finally decided to attack the French and Austrian forces in the west. The two sides met at Rossbach on November 5.

The Battle of Kolin on June 18, 1757, was a setback for the Prussian army of Frederick the Great. The Austrians beat Frederick's army and forced him to give up the siege of Prague.

The Battle of Rossbach was fought on November 5, 1757, between Prussian and Austro-French armies. The 21,000 Prussians, although facing 64,000 French and Austrians, won a major victory.

The Battle of Rossbach opened with the vastly superior Austrians and French sending a huge column, some 40,000 men, to get behind Frederick's left flank. Frederick responded immediately. He moved his entire army, just 21,000 men, south and turned it through 90 degrees. When the slower-moving enemy was able to launch a flank attack, Frederick was ready, facing them head on. Prussian fire mowed down the advancing enemy. This was followed by a Prussian cavalry charge.

Frederick finished off the enemy by an attack with his highly disciplined infantry. Less than 90 minutes after the battle started it was over. For the loss of less than 600 casualties, Frederick had inflicted over 10,000 casualties on the French and Austrians.

Frederick the Great's masterpiece

Frederick did not rest on his laurels after Rossbach—there were other invaders to deal with. His chief concern was Silesia in southern Prussia. A large Austrian force had already defeated a Prussian army on November 22 at Breslau. Frederick marched his men hard, covering 170 miles (272 km) in just 12 days to link up with the troops that had escaped the defeat at Breslau. Frederick had a little over 30,000 men to take on 65,000 Austrians.

The two forces met at Leuthen on December 6. The Austrians deployed over a distance of five miles (8 km), with cavalry on both flanks and the bulk of their reserves on the left. A marsh protected their right. What followed was a stunning Prussian victory. Frederick totally outmaneuvered the Austrians. The Austrians lost 7,000 men killed and wounded, and 12,000 men and over 100 cannon were captured.

THE SEVEN YEARS WAR

THE BATTLE OF LEUTHEN

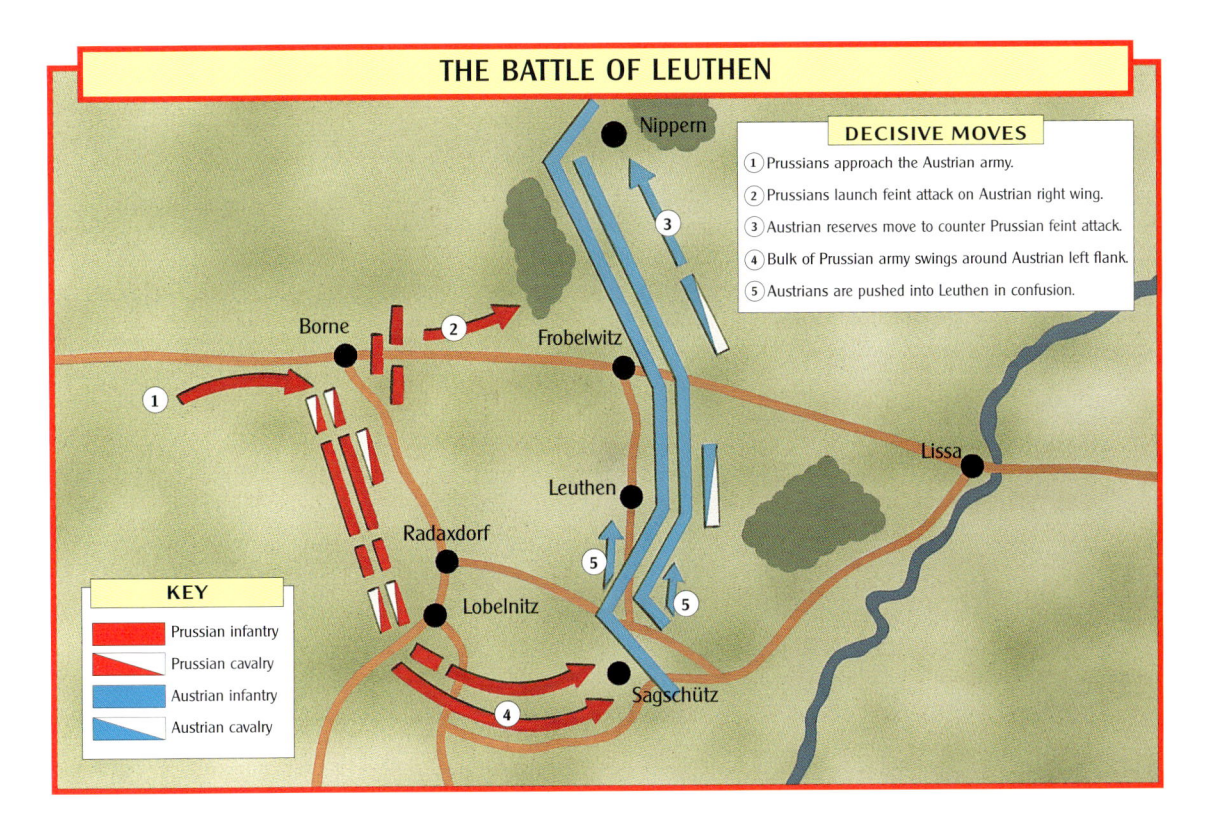

DECISIVE MOVES
1. Prussians approach the Austrian army.
2. Prussians launch feint attack on Austrian right wing.
3. Austrian reserves move to counter Prussian feint attack.
4. Bulk of Prussian army swings around Austrian left flank.
5. Austrians are pushed into Leuthen in confusion.

KEY
- Prussian infantry
- Prussian cavalry
- Austrian infantry
- Austrian cavalry

Frederick pressed his advantage over the Austrians by attacking Austrian territory in May 1758. However, he was forced to abandon the siege of Olmütz on July 1 and attack the Russians, who were menacing eastern Prussia. Moving at speed, he arrived close to Kustrin, which was under siege by 45,000 Russians, in mid-August. Frederick undertook a dangerous crossing of the Oder River at night and got behind the Russians.

The Russians had no option but to fight. The Battle of Zorndorf on the 25th saw 45,000 Russians pitted against Frederick's 36,000 men. Frederick tried to turn the Russian right flank and then the left. The Russians proved stubborn in defense. It was only the charges of Frederick's cavalry under General Frederick Wilhelm von Seydlitz that decided the day. The Russians collapsed. About 19,000 Russians fell, while Frederick lost some 12,000 troops. The threat to eastern Prussia was over.

Frederick had no time to rest. He had to move against a large Austrian army that was menacing much smaller Prussian forces in Saxony. His army covered over 20 miles (32 km) per day. The Prussians caught the Austrians at Hochkirch on October 14. In

The Battle of Leuthen was Frederick's finest victory. Frederick sent the bulk of his army in a wide flanking march that wholly deceived the Austrian commander.

59

Warfare in the 18th Century

Smoke rises over the battlefield at Hochkirch on October 14, 1758. Frederick's Prussians were almost surrounded but were able to cut a path through the Austrian army. Nevertheless, the battle was a major setback for Frederick.

FREDERICK THE GREAT

Frederick the Great of Prussia was a military giant, a leader widely seen as one of the best generals of all time. Frederick's father, Frederick William I, was a brutal man and his son had a very unhappy childhood. On one occasion Frederick was put in prison under suspended sentence of death by his father.

In 1732 Frederick entered the army and soon displayed the qualities that marked him out as a great general. His army was excellent. His infantrymen were harshly disciplined and could move like lightning both before and during a battle. They repeatedly took heavy losses, casualties that would have sent other forces streaming from the battlefield. Yet they stood and fought on. His cavalrymen were equally disciplined and led by a number of talented commanders.

Above all Frederick was a brilliant strategist. He knew that the multinational forces he faced were numerically strong but would find it difficult to combine against him in overwhelming numbers. He believed, usually rightly, that he could defeat each one in turn. Yet he was never able to defeat them entirely. They could always replace their casualties. However, as the war dragged on Frederick was forced to scrape the bottom of the barrel for fresh recruits.

THE SEVEN YEARS WAR

The Seven Years War was fought across much of central Europe. The Prussians were outnumbered by a coalition of countries. However, Frederick the Great of Prussia was often able to move his smaller army at great speed and defeat his opponents before they could unite against him in strength.

the battle that followed Frederick came close to disaster. The 80,000 Austrians were able to surround the 30,000 Prussians during the night and their dawn attack almost succeeded in smashing Frederick's army.

Frederick did manage to regain his initiative over the Austrians by the end of the year, but he had suffered enormous casualties since the war began. While his army was still the finest in all Europe, it was slowly but surely declining in quality—and quantity. When the spring of 1759 arrived he would have to campaign hard to protect Prussia once again.

The French allowed to escape

The 1759 campaign began with an Anglo-Prussian offensive against the French around Frankfurt-am-Main. Then, the Battle of Minden, fought on August 1, should have been a victory for the Anglo-Prussian army. The British infantry fought with great valor to make a crushing victory a real possibility. However, the British cavalry, or rather their commander, Lord Sackville, failed to deliver the decisive charge. The French, who were facing disaster, were allowed to escape. The Prussian commander, Duke Ferdinand of Brunswick, did pursue the French but stopped when some of his troops were recalled by Frederick.

Frederick had problems in the east. Russian forces had defeated a small Prussian army on July 23 and then linked up with the Austrians. These two armies, about 80,000 men, were poised to advance deeper into eastern Prussia. Frederick led his 50,000 men against them. He crossed the Oder River and planned a daring twin-pronged attack on August 12.

Frederick in despair

The Battle of Kunersdorf was a disaster for the Prussians. Their two attacks were thrown back with heavy losses. Frederick displayed some of the stubbornness that was probably his greatest weakness—he continued to attack, thereby adding to an already desperate situation. When Frederick finally saw that he could not defeat the Austro-Russian army, some 19,000 of his best troops had been frittered away.

Frederick was shattered, he had lost the cream of his army, and considered stepping down from his throne. He was lucky to escape pursuit by the Austro-Russian forces, which were equally

Austrian heavy cavalry attacks disorganized Prussian infantry during the Battle of Kunersdorf, August 12, 1759. The Prussians suffered heavy casualties in what was Frederick the Great's worst defeat.

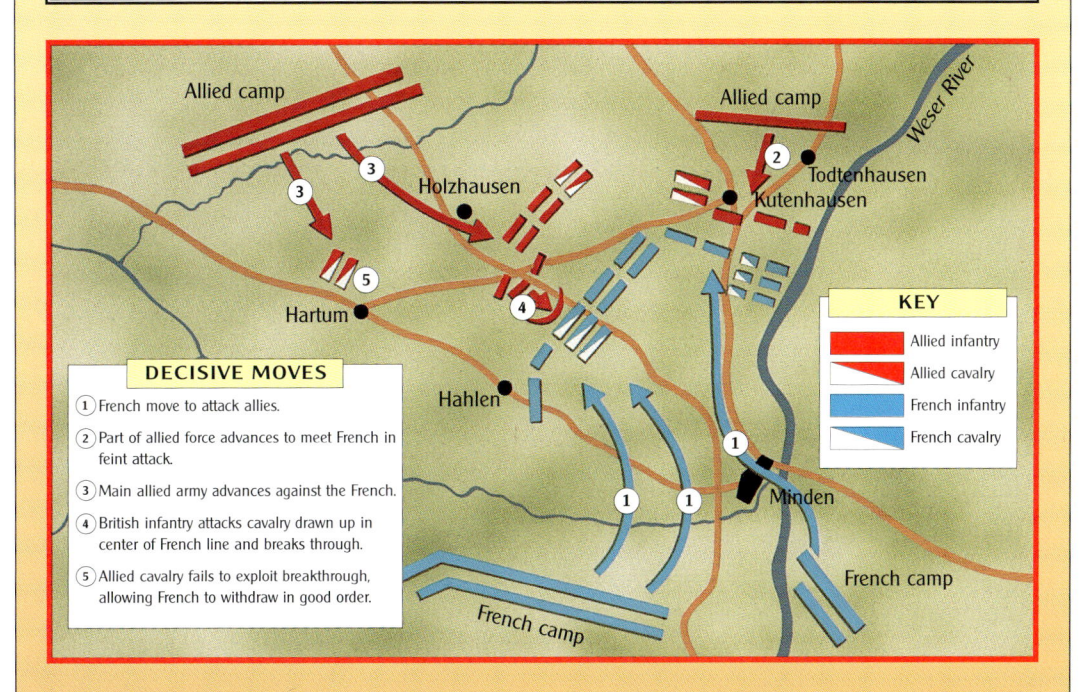

THE BATTLE OF MINDEN

DECISIVE MOVES
1. French move to attack allies.
2. Part of allied force advances to meet French in feint attack.
3. Main allied army advances against the French.
4. British infantry attacks cavalry drawn up in center of French line and breaks through.
5. Allied cavalry fails to exploit breakthrough, allowing French to withdraw in good order.

KEY
- Allied infantry
- Allied cavalry
- French infantry
- French cavalry

The Battle of Minden, fought on August 1, 1759, saw 60,000 French troops pitted against an Anglo-Prussian force of 45,000. The Anglo-Prussian commander, the Duke of Brunswick, launched an attack against the French wing with only a small part of his men. The French met it with overwhelming force and inflicted severe losses on the Anglo-Prussian attackers.

The Duke of Brunswick planned to move reinforcement to help his men but was delayed, allowing the French to keep up the pressure. A desperate measure was called for. Three of Brunswick's brigades marched out to confront the French cavalry in the center. These troops, less than 4,500 men, but including many of the finest regiments in the British army,

The Battle of Minden was a victory for an Anglo-Prussian army over the French. However, it could have been much more decisive if the British cavalry had charged when the French were close to collapse.

repulsed French cavalry charges and stood up to intense artillery fire at close range. They then went in with bayonets. The French center fell apart.

The Anglo-Prussian army was at the point of victory but its British cavalry refused to attack. The French escaped but left 10,000 casualties and over 100 cannon on the field of battle. Brunswick's brave infantry suffered 25 percent casualties in their attack against the French center.

shattered by the fighting. They had suffered over 15,000 casualties. Frederick recovered from the black mood brought about by the defeat at Kunersdorf and regained some of his previous vigor.

In the late summer and early winter of 1759 Frederick rebuilt his main army, gathering new recruits and drawing off some units from those of his other commanders. He also had a little luck. The Russians were forced to abandon the positions in eastern Prussia due to a shortage of supplies. With them out of the way and with a new army at his back, Frederick moved against the Austrians once again. His target was the force of Marshal Leopold von Daun, which had captured Dresden in September.

Frederick at bay

Frederick did not lead the attack on the Austrians in person. He sent one of his generals, Frederick von Finck, to do the job. Later it was clear than von Finck's forces had been far too small to do the task Frederick intended. This was proved the case at the Battle of Maxen, on November 21. The Prussians were smashed by the Austrians, who had concentrated over 40,000 men against them. Frederick's fortunes had reached their lowest level so far.

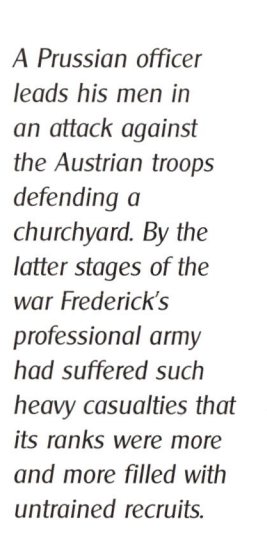

A Prussian officer leads his men in an attack against the Austrian troops defending a churchyard. By the latter stages of the war Frederick's professional army had suffered such heavy casualties that its ranks were more and more filled with untrained recruits.

Frederick's Prussian Army

The Prussian army of Frederick the Great was a well-oiled fighting machine. At its core were the infantrymen. Able to march into battle and fight with parade-ground precision, they were renowned for being able to move rapidly and change their position at great speed even when under fire. They were also able to fire faster than many other infantry units because of their excellent training.

Frederick's cavalry was used in large units, rather than being dispersed throughout the battle line. Their main weapon was the sword. In battle the Prussian cavalry usually charged in two or three ranks and attacked almost shoulder to shoulder. The shock of the impact was often sufficient to scatter an unprepared enemy unit.

Frederick also made sure that his army was not dependent on supply bases. His soldiers carried rations for three days and could be resupplied by the wagon trains that accompanied each regiment. The army as a whole also had a wagon train.

Soldiers serving with the Prussian army of Frederick the Great in the Seven Years War.

It was fortunate for Frederick that Maxen had been fought so late in the campaigning season. With winter setting in, both sides ended their military operations. Prussia's enemies, however, used the winter to plan Frederick's defeat.

By the spring of 1760 an Austrian army of 100,000 men under von Daun was in Saxony. Another 50,000 Austrians led by General Gideon von Loudon were in Silesia, and there were an equal number of Russians in eastern Prussia. Swedish and Russian forces were poised to sweep through Pomerania. The plan was based on the belief that Frederick was not powerful enough to take on all of these forces at the same time. If he concentrated on one then the others would be free to march on Berlin.

Frederick faced von Daun's Austrians and had about 40,000 men under his command. There were about 35,000 Prussian troops protecting Silesia and another 15,000 were located in the north to protect Pomerania. The Duke of Brunswick had 70,000 men but faced over 120,000 French troops in the west. The Duke of Brunswick outwitted the French and was able to push them back to the Rhine. However, he suffered a defeat on October 16 that brought his offensive to a halt. While the Duke of Brunswick was keeping the French occupied, Frederick campaigned in the east. From June to late July he rushed from one threatened point to another.

Frederick was desperate to regain his position. He decided to plunge into Silesia. Driving his army of about 30,000 men hard, he was able to confront the Austrians at Liegnitz on August 15. The Austrians could muster 60,000 men and were expecting the arrival of 30,000 Russians. Frederick realized that the Austrian army was divided into two unequal halves. He chose to attack the weaker part. Under cover of dark he marched against the 24,000 Austrians led personally by Loudon. Loudon realized he had been outmaneuvered but chose to attack.

Loudon's attack failed and Frederick's badly mauled his forces. The Prussians then fell back, aware that the Austrian force of Daun was advancing in their direction. Frederick tried a little trickery to outwit the Russians. He sent a bogus message to the Russians that suggested the entire Austrian army had been defeated at Liegnitz. The ruse worked and the Russians retreated.

Frederick planned to take on Daun's Austrians but discovered that Berlin had been captured on October 9 and partly destroyed. He hurried north to save the situation. The move worked, but the Austrians now concentrated their forces at Torgau. Frederick decided to attack the Austrians at Torgau.

An ambitious attack

The two sides were of roughly equal size, about 50,000 men. Frederick planned an ambitious attack. He would lead one half of his army around the right wing of the Austrian army and strike from the rear. The other half was ordered to make a frontal assault at the same time as Frederick attacked.

The beginning of the Prussian frontal attack was seen by Austrian troops and an exchange of musket fire occurred. Frederick mistakenly thought that the noise of the firing indicated that the main frontal attack was being made. He chose to attack himself but the fighting was inconclusive. The Prussian frontal attack finally got to grips with the Austrians at dusk and Frederick renewed his efforts. The Austrians broke, but Frederick had 17,000 men killed, wounded, or taken prisoner.

The war began again in the spring of 1761. Frederick could muster about 100,000 men but was opposed by 300,000 Austrians and Russians in Silesia. Frederick took up an almost attack-proof defensive position. The Austrians and Russians abandoned their campaign as winter set in. Frederick, however, lost the support of his British allies in December. A new British king, George III, called most of his army in Germany home.

The new year, 1762, brought some better news. The Russian ruler, Empress Elizabeth, died and was replaced by Peter III. Peter respected Frederick and agreed to a peace treaty on May 15. Sweden also agreed to sign the Treaty of Hamburg on May 22. Frederick was free to concentrate on Austria and France.

The Duke of Brunswick's Anglo-Prussian army beat the French at Wilhelmstal on June 24. Frederick matched this by defeating the Austrians at Burkersdorf on July 21. Another Prussian army beat the Austrians at Freiberg on October 29.

Prussian power confirmed

These victories could not hide the fact that all of the warring nations were exhausted by the conflict. An armistice was agreed upon in November and the Treaty of Hubertusburg was signed on February 16, 1763. Austria accepted that Prussia had a right to control Silesia. Frederick had fought for seven years and won many victories and his legacy was to make Prussia a dominant power in central Europe and a key player in European affairs. However, his long war had left his once great army virtually destroyed and left much of Prussia in ruins.

Prussian infantrymen attack Austrian fortifications during the Battle of Torgau on November 3, 1760. The Prussians defeated the Austrians, but the price was high. Frederick's Prussians suffered more than 16,000 casualties.

THE NEW NAVIES

The first 50 years of the 18th century saw little change in the conduct of naval warfare. Admirals and captains were not expected to show any great personal initiative and their conduct before and during a battle was often determined by a rigid set of rules. However, by the end of the century the British navy had developed a level of seamanship and a flexibility of leadership that made its captains masters of the world's oceans. This naval strength was absolutely vital to protect Britain's growing empire around the globe.

One of only two British vessels lost beating the French at the Battle of Quiberon Bay in 1759 founders on a reef. The battle demonstrated that the British were developing more flexible naval tactics.

Before the middle of the century new methods of naval tactics were not encouraged. The world's navies followed a standard battle plan. In line ahead, one ship sailing behind another, two enemy fleets would near each other to close range and the individual warships would then each pick out a rival vessel and exchange volleys. Whichever ship could survive the exchange of gunfire the longer was usually the victor.

The two greatest navies of the age were the British and French. The British had the greater number of ships and were, in general, the better sailors. The French had the better ships, although they did not handle them as well. The British tended to be the more aggressive in action. At the Battle of Quiberon Bay off the west coast of France in 1759, at the height of the Seven Years War, a British fleet led by Admiral Edward Hawke defeated a French fleet. The French believed that Hawke would not risk sailing his ships through reef-strewn waters in rough seas to attack them. Hawke did just this and sank seven French warships.

The French did have one outstanding naval officer in the 18th century. Admiral Pierre André de Suffren fought in the War of the Austrian Succession, the Seven Years War, and the American Revolution. He was a bold commander who also had a fine tactical and strategic mind that allowed him to outfox and defeat his often more numerous opponents.

Warship design

The warships built by the two rivals were very similar. They were sail-powered, and each carried a variable number of cannon that lay in tiers, one above another, on either side of the ship. The bigger the ship, the greater the number of tiers and cannon. The biggest vessels, known as first-raters, carried over 100 cannon, while the smaller fifth- or sixth-raters had around 16 or 20.

Ship design did not change a great deal during the century. However, there were two new developments that greatly improved a ship's seaworthiness. First, there was the introduction of copper bottoms to the underwater section of the hull. Oak was frequently eaten away by a marine worm—the teredo—and copper sheeting was an ideal solution to a costly problem. Second, the tiller, which had been used to steer a ship's rudder, was replaced by a series of cables and pulleys attaching the rudder to a steering wheel. This new system made steering less tiring and made the vessel much more maneuverable.

Questions of aggression

Because of the rigid instructions under which commanders fought—and the penalties they faced if they broke them—French captains, afraid of losing ships, tended to be less aggressive. Their British counterparts, with their greater numbers, were expected to seek out and destroy the enemy "by the book." Any lack of aggression could be punished heavily.

One unfortunate British commander in the Seven Years War is a case in point. Admiral Sir John Byng was attempting to break the French siege of Port Mahon, the capital of the Mediterranean island of Minorca. He faced a French fleet of equal strength on May 20, 1756, but had difficulty in bringing his warships into the required line ahead formation.

The French took advantage of this and severely damaged a number of Byng's ships before escaping. Byng realized that he had no hope of helping Port Mahon and returned to the British base at Gibraltar in southern Spain. Byng was court-martialed. He was found guilty and executed.

New ideas

Given such punishments it is perhaps surprising that sticking to the strict code of conduct in battle was swept away in the second half of the century. Part of the reason for this was that a band of aggressive young British naval officers ignored the accepted procedures and won major victories. Among these was Admiral George Rodney, whose victory over the French at the Battle of the Saintes fought off the Caribbean island of Dominica in 1782 could not prevent Britain's defeat in the American Revolution.

The young officers recognized that the old line ahead system, in which one ship followed another, left a great deal to chance. They believed it better to adopt a formation that would allow several ships to "gang up" on a single—or fewer—enemy vessels.

The answer lay in giving up the parallel lines of warships. It was thought that a British fleet would do better to approach the enemy ships at an angle of 90 degrees, break through the enemy

British Admiral Sir John Byng is executed after being found guilty of "neglect of duty in battle" by a court martial. Byng was, in fact, a scapegoat for the probably unavoidable loss of the Mediterranean island of Minorca to the French during the Seven Years War.

Red-hot Cannon Fire

In September 1782 the British defenders of Gibraltar on the south coast of Spain, who had been under siege by the French and Spanish for three years, tried to smash a number of heavily protected warships. Their cannonballs just bounced off the ships' massive wooden timbers. The British tried something very different.

They heated up their cannonballs, carried the hot rounds to their cannon using tongs, and them rammed them home. The gunpowder in the barrels did not explode because damp wads were placed between the gunpowder and the red-hot shot.

Over 8,000 of the special cannonballs were fired on September 12. By the following day all of the enemy's warships had been burned to the waterline or had exploded. The danger had passed and the British garrison, although exhausted and close to starvation, survived until supplies arrived in October.

Red-hot shot is used to destroy several French warships at Gibraltar.

battle line, and then the British ships could maneuver in small groups, concentrating their firepower against one or two enemy vessels. The tactic demanded that the captain or admiral of the lead ship had a cool nerve.

The British made improvements in gunnery that increased the firepower they could use on an enemy. One of these was the introduction of a block-and-tackle system for aiming individual guns. This allowed guns to change direction to either the left or right, making it easier for them to fire at ships not quite in the direct line of sight.

New battle tactics, improvements in both ship construction and firepower, and a new style of imaginative leadership made sure that Britain had the world's finest navy by the end of the century. When Britain was menaced by the ships of Napoleon Bonaparte and his European allies, it had the ships, commanders, and crews it needed.

CATHERINE THE GREAT'S WARS

German-born Catherine II, known today as Catherine the Great, ascended the Russian throne in 1762 after her husband, Peter III, had been deposed by his nobles and senior generals. He had been on the throne for less than six months. Catherine ruled until 1796. During her reign she went to war with Poland, had to deal with international rivals in Europe, and further weakened the power of the already declining Ottoman Turkish Empire in the Balkans. Catherine made Russia one of Europe's leading powers.

Empress Catherine the Great of Russia was a tough ruler. She waged numerous wars against neighboring states to make Russia a leading power.

Catherine's first major military adventure was against a group of rebellious Polish nobles known as the Confederation of the Bar. They opposed Russia's growing political involvement in Poland and objected to their own government, which was pro-Russian. The rebellion, which began in 1768, was put down by a Russian army, but the rebels had called on Turkey to help them by declaring war on the Russians.

Russia attacks Turkey

In October 1768 war was declared. The Turks had, in fact, ignored the Polish rebels' calls to help them. However, Russian troops chased some of the rebel Poles into Turkish territory and destroyed a Turkish town, provoking Turkey to declare war. The Russian army moved rapidly, defeating the Turks in the Caucasus and then invading the Balkans in 1769. The Russian commander, Count Peter Rumiantsev, smashed a Turkish army on the Dniester River, took the town of Jassy, and then conquered the Turkish-held provinces of Moldavia and Wallachia.

To keep the Turks off balance, the Russians backed revolts in both Egypt and Greece (both controlled by Turkey) in 1769 and 1770. The Greek rebellion was brutally put down by the Turks, but the Russians soon had better news. At the naval Battle of Chesme, fought on July 6, 1770, off the Mediterranean coast of Turkey, a Russian fleet led by Admiral Aleksei Orlov overwhelmed a Turkish fleet. Even better news came in August. Rumiantsev, taking advantage of his victory on the Dniester, was able to defeat a Turkish force that had been mustered to eject him from Moldavia.

In 1771 the Russians continued to expand their territory by making further conquests. Prince Vasily Dolgoruky advanced into the Crimea, taking over the peninsula. The Turks, battered by the run of defeats between 1769 and 1771, opened peace negotiations in 1772. However, this was a trick. The drawn-out talks allowed them to build fresh armies. War broke out again in 1773, but the Turks met with further disasters. Rumiantsev moved south from his position along the Danube River against the main Turkish field army, which fell back on Shulma.

Another Russian general, Alexander Suvarov, tackled the Turks at Shulma in June 1774 and won a famous victory. War-weariness was setting in and the Treaty of Kuchuk Kainarji was signed on July 16. Russia returned some of the territories it had

The Battle of Chesme was fought between Russian and Turkish fleets off the Mediterranean coast of Asia Minor (modern Turkey) on July 6, 1770. The Russian admiral, Aleksei Orlov, was victorious.

WARFARE IN THE 18TH CENTURY

ALEXANDER SUVAROV

Suvarov was the greatest Russian commander of the second half of the 18th century. He fought in virtually all of Russia's wars from the Seven Years War in 1756 to the War of the French Revolution in the final years of the century. He was made Count Rimniksky for his triumph against the Turks in 1789 and was later promoted to field marshal.

Despite his string of military victories, Suvarov was sent into retirement when Czar Paul III came to the throne. He did not appreciate Suvarov's reforms, which included better pay and conditions for his men. However, Suvarov was recalled to service when Russia joined in the war against Revolutionary France.

Suvarov fought against the French in Italy and won three major battles against them in 1799. He was nevertheless removed from command in 1800. Paul III took away his much-deserved titles and honors. Suvarov died a broken man the same year. It was a cruel end for one of Russia's finest soldiers.

General Suvarov rides into Warsaw, the Polish capital, in 1794 after defeating a Polish rebellion.

---

captured to the Turks but, more importantly, gained two points of access to the Black Sea, a stretch of water whose coastline had been dominated by the Turks.

The peace last for 14 years. The Russians, eager to expand their rule, intrigued to gain control over Georgia. The Turks tried to encourage the Crimean tribes to rebel against their Russian overlords. In 1788 Suvarov defeated the Turks at Kinburn, thereby preventing them from liberating the Crimea.

The Russians also enjoyed considerable success in a number of naval actions. John Paul Jones, the American hero, led the Russian fleet into action at the two Battles of Liman in June

1788. In the second battle the Turks lost 15 ships and 3,000 men. Jones, displaying his seafaring skills to the full, had just one ship sunk and only 18 men killed.

The focus of the war switched to Moldavia in 1789. With the support of Austrian allies, who invaded from the west, the Russians advanced from the north. Some of the advances were unsuccessful, but a united Russian and Austrian army, of which Suvarov held joint command, was resoundingly successful. Two battles in the summer—particularly one at Focsani on August 1—badly damaged the Turks. Suvarov continued his advance and forced the Turks to fall back to the Danube River.

Further Russian victories

The Austrians and Russians enjoyed other victories in 1789. One Austrian general, Gideon von Laudon, successfully opposed a Turkish attack in the Balkans and then went on to take Belgrade (now the capital of Yugoslavia). The Turks were alarmed by this turn of events and sought to negotiate a peace treaty with Austria. This was agreed on in 1791. Austria returned Belgrade to Turkish control but kept part of the Balkans.

Catherine the Great's armies concentrated on pushing the borders of the growing Russian Empire westward. The two main areas of operations were in Poland and against the Turkish forces in the Balkans and Black Sea area.

The Turks had to deal with a revolt in Greece in 1790 that severely undermined their ability to concentrate their efforts on defeating the Russians. Worse was to follow. On December 22, Suvarov captured the important fortress of Ismail at the mouth of the Danube. When the fortress fell Suvarov ordered the massacre of all its Turkish defenders. He was promoted to the rank of field marshal for the capture of Ismail.

Poland dismembered

Despite these victories the Russians themselves were eager to reach a peace agreement with the Turks. This was due to problems in Poland, where the Prussians were trying to increase their political influence. The Treaty of Jassy was signed on January 9, 1792. The Russians returned Moldavia and Bessarabia to the Turks but kept hold of the territories they had captured that lay to the east of the Dniester.

Russia invaded Poland and Prussia did likewise to prevent all of Poland coming under Russian control. The two powers agreed to carve Poland up between them, a move that caused the Poles to rebel in 1794. The small Polish forces were commanded by Thaddeus Kosciusko, who had played a major part fighting for the colonists in the American Revolution.

Kosciusko's military experience initially paid off. He defeated a small Russian force in April (2,000 of his soldiers were armed with no more than pitchforks and scythes) but against the might of much larger Prussian and Russian forces he was forced back to Warsaw, the capital, which was placed under siege in late August. The heavily outnumbered Poles, some 35,000 soldiers with 200 artillery guns, defended their capital with great valor, defeating two major assaults by the Prussian and Russian armies whose combined strength was some 100,000 troops and 250 guns. The siege was defeated by the Poles at the beginning of September.

Russia's rise to power

The Polish victory at Warsaw was short-lived, however. Kosciusko, with just 7,000 troops, was decisively defeated by a 16,000-strong Russian army at the Battle of Maciejowice, a little way south of the capital, on October 10. Kosciusko was wounded during the battle and then captured. Without his inspired leadership the Polish rebellion quickly collapsed. Poland disappeared as an independent country in 1795 and Russia became one of the dominant powers in Eastern Europe.

Polish patriot Thaddeus Kosciusko falls from his horse after being wounded at the Battle of Maciejowice in 1794.

Russia had also fought a war against Sweden between 1788 and 1790. The Swedes began the war believing that the Russians were intent on invading Sweden. Despite two early defeats, the Swedes recovered sufficiently to take on the Russian navy in July 1790. The battle left the Russian fleet in tatters—53 ships were sunk by the Swedes. Peace between Russia and Sweden swiftly followed, on August 15, 1790.

Catherine's reign saw Russia become a major player in European affairs. Due to the many wars fought in Catherine's reign, Russia had extended its territories deeper into Eastern Europe, gained access to the Black Sea, reduced Turkish power in the Balkans, and taken over a portion of Poland. Russia, however, would soon become involved in the Napoleonic Wars and have to fight for its survival.

GLOSSARY

column A type of military formation in which the depth of the unit (number of ranks of men) is greater than its width.

line A type of military formation in which a unit is strung out in a line of between two and four ranks of troops deep.

militia Civilians who have undergone a degree of usually yearly military training. They were most often called into action in time of national or local emergency.

morale How a soldier feels. Soldiers with high morale are likely to fight better than those with low morale. Levels of morale can be influenced by training, confidence in officers, the quality and supply of food, health, and degree of tiredness.

musket The standard infantry firearm. The musket was loaded by ramming a musket ball down the barrel and then taking aim. The weapon was fired by pulling the trigger, which released a piece of flint down into a pan primed with gunpowder. This ignited, in turn igniting the gunpowder in the cartridge in the barrel and propelling the ball toward its target.

rifle A type of musket with a higher degree of accuracy and greater range. The key difference from a standard weapon was rifling (grooves) cut into the barrel. These groves gave spin to a musket ball as it traveled down the barrel, leading to better and more accurate shooting.

shrapnel A type of explosive cannonball developed by Englishman Henry Shrapnel in 1784. His cannonball consisted of a iron shell filled with musket balls and an explosive charge, which burst in the air after firing at a target.

skirmishers Infantrymen trained to fight in open order rather than the closed ranks of ordinary soldiers. Their role was to prepare the way for the main attack by sniping at the enemy and its officers, or to disorganize any enemy counterattack.

BIBLIOGRAPHY

Note: *An asterisk (*) denotes a Young Adult title.*

*Averill, Esther H. *King Philip, the Indian Chief.* Linnet Books, 1993

*Brownstone, David, and Franck, Irene. *Timelines of Warfare From 100,000 B.C. to the Present.* Little, Brown and Company, 1994

Chandler, David. *The Art of Warfare in the Age of Marlborough.* Sarpedon Publishers, 1997

*Cobb, Hubbard. *American Battlefields: A Complete Guide to the Historic Conflicts in Words, Maps, and Photos.* Konecky and Konecky, 1995

*Duffy, Christopher. *The Army of Frederick the Great.* Emperor's Press, 1996

*Duffy, Christopher. *Fire and Stone: The Science of Fortress Warfare, 1660–1860.* Stackpole Books, 1996

Dupuy, R. Ernest and Dupuy, Trevor. *The Collins Encyclopedia of Military History.* HarperCollins, 1993

Dupuy, R.E., Johnson, Curt, and Bongard, David L. *The Harper Encyclopedia of Military Biography.* HarperCollins, 1995

Mitchison, Rosalind. *A History of Scotland.* Routledge, 1997

*McGuire, Leslie. *Catherine the Great.* Chelsea House, 1996

Nosworthy, Brian. *The Anatomy of Victory: Battle Tactics, 1689–1763.* Hippocrene, 1990

*Ochoa, George. *The Fall of Quebec and the French and Indian War.* Silver Burdett Press, 1996

William, Noel St. John. *Redcoats Along the Hudson: The Struggle for North America, 1754–63.* Brassey's Inc., 1997

INDEX

Numbers in *italics* refer to illustrations.

Amherst, Jeffrey, 43, 44
Anglo–French Wars, 39–47, *41*
Anne, queen of England, 21, 23
Austria,
  Catherine the Great's wars, 72–77, *75*
  Seven Years War, 56–62, *61*, 64–67
  War of the Austrian Succession, 24–31, *25*
  War of the Spanish Succession, 12–23, *21*

Battles, major,
  Blenheim, 14–16, *15*
  Chesme, 73, *73*
  Culloden, *32*, 33
  Denain, 22, *22*
  Dettingen, 26, *26*
  Fontenoy, 28, *28*, 29, *29*
  Hochkirch, 59–61, *60*
  Hohenfriedberg, 30, *30*, *31*
  Kolin 56–57, *57*
  Kunersdorf, 62, *62*, 64
  Lake George, 40, *40*
  Leuthen, 58, *59*
  Malplaquet, 20, *20*
  Minden, 61–62, *63*, *63*
  Monongahela, 39, *39*
  Narva, 5, *6*, 7
  Plassey, 51, 52, *52*, 53, *53*
  Poltava, 8–10, *10*, 11, *11*
  Porto Novo, 54, *54*
  Quebec, 44–47, *46*, *47*
  Quiberon Bay, *68*, 69
  Ramillies, 16–17, *16*
  Rossbach, 58, *58*
  Ticonderoga, 43–44, *43*, *45*
  Torgau, 66, 67, *67*
Black Hole of Calcutta, 51, *51*
Bohemia, 25, 26, 30, 56–57
Britain,
  India, Anglo–French struggle for, 48–55, *55*
  Jacobite Rebellions 32–33, *32*
  Native American wars, 34–37, *37*
  navy, 68–71
  North America, Anglo–French Wars, 38–47, *41*
  Queen Anne's War, 23
  Seven Years War, 56–57, 61, 62, 63, *63*
  War of the Austrian Succession, 25, 26, 28, 29, 31
  War of the Spanish Succession, 13–23, *21*
Byng, Admiral Sir John, 69–70, *70*

Canada, 38, 40, 41, 43–47
Catherine the Great, 72, *72*, 77
Charles XII (of Sweden), 5–11, *5*
Clive, Robert, 48–53, *48*, *52*
Cumberland, Duke of, 28, 29, 33

Denmark, 5, 10, 11
Dupleix, Marquis Joseph, 48, 49, 50

Eugene, Prince of Austria, 12–23, *12*

France, 34
  India, Anglo-French struggle for, 48–55, 52, 54
  navy, 68–71
  North America, Anglo–French wars, 38–47
  Queen Anne's War, 23
  Seven Years War, 56–58, 61–63
  War of the Austrian Succession, 25, 26, 27, 28, 29, 31
  War of the Spanish Succession, 12–23
Frederick the Great, 4, 24, 25, 27–28, 30, 31, *31*, 56–67, *56*
  army, 60, *64*, 65, *65*

Great Northern War, 5–11

India, Anglo–French struggle for, 4, 48–55
Italy, 12–13, 17, 23

Jacobite Rebellions, 32–33, *32*

Kosciusko, Thaddeus, 76, *77*

Maria Theresa, 24, *24*, 25, 31
Marlborough, Duke of, 4, 13–21, *16*, *18*
Moldavia, 73, 75, 76
Montcalm, Marquis Louis Joseph de, 41–46, *45*

Native Americans, *1*, 34–37, *34*, *36*, *37*
naval warfare, 68–71, *71*
Netherlands, 13, 25, 26, 28, 31, 34, *see also* Spanish Netherlands
North America, 4
  Anglo–French Wars, 38–47
  Native American wars, 34–37, *37*
  Queen Anne's War, 23

Peter the Great of Russia, 5, 6, 7, *7*, 8, 9, 10
Poland,
  Great Northern War, 5, 6, 10
  Russia's wars with, 72, 76, 77
Pontiac, chief of the Ottawa, 36–37
Protestants,
  Jacobite Rebellions, 32–33, *32*
Prussia, 13
  army, 60, *61*, 65, *65*
  Seven Years War, 56–57
  War of the Austrian Succession, 24, 25, 27–28, 30–31

Quebec, 44–47, *46*, *47*

Rogers' Rangers, 42, *42*
Russia,
  Catherine the Great's wars, 72–77
  Great Northern War, 5–11

Seven Years War, 56–57, 59, 62, 64–67

Saxe, Marshal Maurice de, 26–27, *27*, 28, *28*, 29
Saxony, 24, 25, 28, 56, 59, 65
Scotland, Jacobite Rebellions, 32–33, *32*
Seven Years War, 56–67
Silesia, 24, 25, 28, 30, 31, 58, 65, 66, 67

Spain, North America, conflict in, 34
War of the Austrian Succession, 24, 27
War of the Spanish Succession, 12, 22–23
Spanish Netherlands, 12, 14, 23
Stuart, Charles Edward, the "Young Pretender," 32–33
Suvarov, Alexander, 73–74, *74*, 75, 76

Sweden, Catherine the Great's war, 77
Great Northern War, 5-11
Seven Years War, 56, 57, 65, 67

Turkey, 10–11, 72–75, 76, 77

War of the Austrian Succession, 24–31, 48
War of the Spanish Succession, 12–23

Washington, George, 38–39, *38*
Wellington, Duke of, 55
Wolfe, James, 43, 44–47

ACKNOWLEDGMENTS

Cover (main picture) AKG Photo, London, (inset) AKG Photo, London; page 1 Peter Newark's Military Pictures; page 5 Peter Newark's Military Pictures; page 6 Hulton Getty Collection; page 7 Peter Newark's Military Pictures; page 9 Mary Evans Picture Library; page 10 AKG Photo, London; page 12 AKG Photo, London/Erich Lessing; page 13 Peter Newark's Historical Pictures; page 16 Hulton Getty Collection; page 18 Peter Newark's Historical Pictures; page 20 Peter Newark's Historical Pictures; page 22 AKG Photo, London; page 24 AKG Photo, London; page 26 Hulton Getty Collection; page 27 AKG Photo, London/Erich Lessing; page 28 AKG Photo, London; page 30 AKG Photo, London; page 31 AKG Photo, London; page 32 Hulton Getty Collection; page 34 Peter Newark's Military Pictures; page 36 Peter Newark's Military Pictures; page 38 Peter Newark's Military Pictures; page 39 Peter Newark's Military Pictures; page 40 Peter Newark's Military Pictures; page 42 Peter Newark's Military Pictures; page 43 Peter Newark's Military Pictures; page 45 Peter Newark's Military Pictures; page 45 Peter Newark's Military Pictures; page 46 Peter Newark's American pictures; page 48 Peter Newark's Historical Pictures; page 51 Peter Newark's Historical Pictures; page 52 Peter Newark's Military Pictures; page 54 Peter Newark's Military Pictures; page 56 AKG Photo, London; page 57 AKG Photo, London; page 58 AKG Photo, London; page 60 AKG Photo, London; page 62 Peter Newark's Military Pictures; page 64 AKG Photo, London; page 65 AKG Photo, London; page 67 AKG Photo, London; page 68 Peter Newark's Military Pictures; page 70 Hulton Getty Collection; page 71 Hulton Getty Collection; page 72 AKG Photo, London; page 73 Hulton Getty Collection; page 74 Peter Newark's Military Pictures: page 77 AKG Photo, London.